Far Away In Time

By

Maria Savva

Published by:

Rose and Freedom Books

P.O. Box 55285

London N22 9EU

England, U.K.

Copyright © Maria Savva 2014

Cover photo by © hotblack - morguefile.com

A catalogue record of this book is available from the British Library

ISBN: 978-0-9928345-0-0

Acknowledgements:

Thanks to my excellent beta readers for your helpful feedback. The book is better because of your suggestions. You have given me food for thought for future short story collections/novels, too, which is great! I'm truly grateful to you all for helping and inspiring me.

Michael Radcliffe
Catherine Rose
Darcia Helle
Danille Eaves Dillon
Laura Smith
Julie Elizabeth Aldridge
Marina Savva

BIG thank you to my proofreader, Susan Buchanan. Thanks for having the same OCD with regard to editing as me! Your help was invaluable. You inspired me to fine tune the stories even more, and I'm grateful for that. Thanks for going above and beyond what was required with the extra editing suggestions.

Thanks to Scott M. Liddell (hotblack on morguefile.com) for letting me use your beautiful photograph for the cover.

The Stories:

The Ghost of Christmas Past

For everyone else it was Christmas. A time of peace. A time for joy, a time for giving, for sharing, and for miracles.

Roland secured the double bolt on the front door and set the alarm. Funny how the code for the alarm was 2512, as if some sort of premonition, or precursor. Adrienne chose it: 'Christmas Day. It's a date we'll remember. I'm rubbish with passwords and don't want to be setting off the alarm all the time!' she'd said.

Roland trundled up the stairs and lay down on the threadbare sheets. *I'll buy some new sheets next time I'm out,* he thought to himself, as he had done plenty of times over the past year. He never did buy any, though, his mind elsewhere.

The curtains could do with a wash, he thought, gazing at the drapes that covered the window shutting out the world beyond. Always closed. It was dark when he left for work in the morning and dark when he got home; no need to draw the curtains.

The tears were a constant companion this late at night. He hardly noticed them. They were a way of life. Night after night, he cried himself to sleep in an empty house once so full of life. Christmas Eve. Here it was again. Christmas Eve.

His mind was blank, no memories were allowed inside, although a hint of a smile threatened to break through whenever he thought of little Rachael and Timmy begging to open their presents early.

'It's Christmas Eve! Come on, Daddy!' pleaded Rachael.

'Go to bed. Santa won't deliver the presents if you're still up when he passes by the house. He knows when you're awake, you know.'

Timmy giggled. 'Santa won't mind.'

The scene played out in Roland's head. His heart reached out to the images of the two children so real in his mind. He could still see Rachael's dimples and unruly red hair, and still hear Timmy's giggle and see the way his tiny nose wrinkled and golden curls danced when he laughed.

Roland stretched out his hand and switched off the bedside lamp, wondering why he was going to bed so early; no need to get up early for work tomorrow, or for the next week. The void of time spread out before him. A feeling of dread surfaced as he contemplated all the hours, the barren days, he'd spend alone with his thoughts.

He absent-mindedly swiped a hand over his face in an attempt to wipe away the tears. His eyes disregarded his actions and continued to pour forth a constant stream as reminders of that day besieged him.

The gunmen had entered the house through the back door. He always thought of them as "gun*men*" even though he'd never seen them.

Adrienne was the type of woman who would stand up for herself, protect her property, her children. She'd shaken Roland awake. 'We've got burglars! There's noise downstairs. Can you hear it?' she whispered. 'Probably opportunists, wanting to take the gifts from under the tree. Bastards. I'll sort them out.' Swinging the bedroom door closed, she pulled her dressing gown from the hook. She left the room, then popped her head round the door. 'Roly, check on the kids, make sure they're all right.'

Roland wiped his eyes. In his half-asleep state he felt too tired to protest, but something urged him to follow her. 'Adrienne! Wait! Anyone could be down there; they might have a knife... might be dangerous!' He sat up and rubbed his eyes again, but she'd gone.

Jumping out of bed, he ran to the top of the stairs.

She stood at the entrance to the living room and let out a raucous cry, 'Noooooooo!'

A shrill sound, like no sound he'd heard before. The sound of sheer terror.

Timmy and Rachael had sneaked downstairs to open their presents. They'd been shot. Adrienne's scream was the sound of a mother watching her children's lives being extinguished. As the memories returned, Roland pulled a pillow over his head wanting to block out the reverberation. The sound echoed even now, twelve months later; had burrowed into his ears, lived there, turned up the volume occasionally. Incessant. He pressed the pillow harder and harder against his head, wanting to suffocate. He couldn't go through with it. *Coward.* The same taunt from his subconscious mind that followed him everywhere.

The shot came quickly. Adrienne fell where she stood. Roland from his vantage point at the top of the stairs heard the gunshot, saw her fall. Blood; lots of blood. Her life was ended. Her last vision the sight of her two children being gunned down. They, the killers—he assumed it was "they", not just one person who had caused such carnage—were still out there. Somewhere. Most nights, he wished, waited, prayed they'd be back to kill him so he could join his family wherever they were.

Then there were the "if onlys". *If only I'd gone downstairs instead of Adrienne... shouldn't have let Adrienne go alone... she'd still be alive. If only I'd let the children open their presents before they went to bed, they wouldn't have had to sneak downstairs... would still be alive. If only I'd gone downstairs when they killed Adrienne. They'd have killed me too. If only.*

He'd called the police, but could do no more. Didn't want

7

to go downstairs to see the bodies.

He was a suspect for a while. *'Funny how he was the only one to survive.'* , *'Why hadn't he gone downstairs; why Adrienne?'*, *'Why would gunmen shoot the children? Much more likely to have been someone they'd known—a crime of passion.'* , *'Were there any domestic arguments prior to the murders?'*.

The speculation and suspicion accentuated his pain, but he blamed himself; he should have died too, or should have saved them. *Coward*. His own mind harboured guilt and remorse. Perhaps it showed.

After months of therapy, he could now sometimes smile at the memories of Adrienne and the children, but could not stop the tears flowing every night, could not quell the flood. In the months following the murders, Roland became increasingly distant from the people he knew. There was no one he could really call a friend anymore. A wall had been built brick by brick, closing him off from his wider circle.

The depression sent him to a different place; a place that the people around him found hard to comprehend. His mood swings, the anger, the silent times. No one knew how to behave in his presence anymore, and they seemed to have decided it wasn't worth trying to find out. He knew there were more than a few of them who wondered: Did he kill Adrienne and the children?

On confronting his best friend, Graham, and his wife, Georgia, three months after the murders—asking why they were not there for him, why they stayed away—he'd grown so irate, so aggressive. He noticed Georgia's face then: the same look the police had when they first questioned him. Had he brutally extinguished three lives that night? The question was there in her eyes, the eyes that could not meet his. Walking away from their house, he felt ashamed of his behaviour. It wasn't worth apologising, though; they wouldn't understand. That was the last time he saw them.

The barriers he put up, and the lack of patience from his former close friends—or their inability to make sense of his change of personality—created a distance and snapped the bridges. His therapist told him his relationships would be healed in time, and went on to say Roland should not feel bad for acting out his anger or taking it out on his friends and family. They would come round eventually; realise that the trauma made him behave differently. They would forgive him. The therapist said the reason they stayed away might be because they did not know how to console him, wanted to let him find his own way to heal, to give him the time he needed; they were unsure what to say to him, didn't want to make him feel worse.

Roland knew they would stay away, though. His so-called friends had labelled him, or at least they had moved on, not wanting this dark cloud hanging over their perfect lives. There would forever be an unspoken element of doubt below the surface. It was his word against the word of a woman and two children who could no longer speak for themselves. They were the victims.

He was a victim, too, but no one seemed to appreciate that.

Work—the one thing he'd moaned about for years— became his saving grace. Those hours in the office away from the house, a fragile normality for eight hours a day, helped him go on.

He slowly drifted off to sleep, once again praying for the gunmen to come back and finish the job, wondering how he would get through the week to come. There would be no escape to the office. The office had closed for Christmas.

*

His alarm clock sounded at 7.30 a.m. He'd forgotten to switch it off the night before. Could that have been a subconscious decision? Had he been hoping against hope that he could go to work, get away from the loneliness, the memories, reluctant to let go of the routine?

Switching off the alarm clock, he sat up in bed. Bells chimed in the distance, no doubt calling people to church for the holy day.

For everyone else it was Christmas.

Far Away In Time - Part I

'The cottage with the purple door that we used to visit.'

'What cottage?' Carrie screwed up her face.

Angie giggled. 'Your memory is so bad, Carrie! How old are you?'

'Um... I'm not the one talking about imaginary cottages with purple doors.'

'But we used to go there every week after school. Mr Silverfrost, the old man with the very white hair and the strange squint. We used to say it looked like he was winking at us.'

'I have no idea what you're on about, Ang.' Carrie shrugged. 'Maybe I have early onset Alzheimer's, or something.'

Angie looked down at her hands. 'I can't believe you've forgotten.'

Carrie gazed at her with a downturned mouth. 'Sorry, don't remember a thing about it. How old was I?'

'Well, I was about nine, so you'd have been about six, I suppose.'

'Hmm... Maybe I was too young to remember.'

Carrie looked at her watch and stood up. 'Listen, Ang, I've

got to go and collect Ivy from school. I wish you didn't live so far from us. Come up on Sunday so the kids can play together. It's been ages since they've seen each other.'

'Okay, sounds good. See you on Sunday,' said Angie, as Carrie waved good-bye.

When she closed the front door, Angie caught sight of herself in the hallway mirror and saw the dejected expression on her face. A kind of gloom had settled following her sister's denial of all knowledge about Mr Silverfrost and the cottage on the corner with the purple door. Carrie was the one person she shared that memory with, but Carrie had forgotten. It filled Angie with a sense of sadness; Mr Silverfrost and the spooky "magic" cottage had been such a big part of her childhood memories.

The next day, Angie left an hour earlier than she usually would to collect the children from school, deciding to take a detour on the way and drive past the old cottage with the purple door. She hadn't visited that part of town since her family moved out over twenty years before.

On the approach to the street where she grew up, Angie slowed the car to observe the surroundings. Everything appeared more or less the same as she remembered it, but *smaller*. Driving along, she noticed how small the front gardens were. They had seemed so big when she was growing up. She'd played in their front garden with Carrie and a couple of friends. Now, it only looked big enough for one, or—at a stretch—two people, to stand in.

Driving past number 54, the old house where she'd lived for five years, she continued along the road and turned left at the end of the street, heading towards the school.

A sense of excitement gripped her and she smiled when the little cottage at the corner of the street came into view. It hadn't changed much at all. *I wonder if Mr Silverfrost still lives here?*

Parking the car outside, she checked the time on the dashboard display, aware that she'd have to collect the children soon.

Her hand trembled as she pressed the key fob to lock the

car, nerves jangling. An odd reaction, but she put it down to not having been here for so long and wondering how Mr Silverfrost would react when he saw her. If he was still here. *He must have been in his sixties at least, back then. He'll be in his eighties or nineties now. If he's still alive.* She shivered at the thought.

Angie hesitated for a moment in front of the purple door. When she finally found the courage to reach for the knocker, the door swung open on its hinges. The interior appeared to be bathed in shadows; Angie assumed that was because her eyes had been dazzled by the sun outside and needed time to adjust.

'Hello,' she called out. There was no reply. Turning back around, and seeing no one out on the street, she shrugged and went inside.

The door slammed shut just after she entered, startling her.

'Don't be alarmed, dear; that door has dodgy springs. I've been meaning to fix it.'

Mr Silverfrost? He was sitting in his brown armchair by the fireplace, as he used to do; his cat, Amber, by his feet. Angie's mouth fell open. *How?* He'd hardly aged at all, and the cat looked the same. Had she somehow travelled back in time?

'It's Angie, isn't it?' He squinted as if in thought. 'I never forget a face. How long since you were last here? Twenty years? You like Ribena with a purple glass and a pink straw, correct?'

Angie could not help but giggle. Her own daughter Ruby was at the age where pink and purple were her favourite colours. 'Um... yes, I remember. You've hardly changed,' she remarked, finding her voice.

'The elixir of youth. Yes. Pity I didn't discover it when I was younger. Now I'm stuck looking like a seventy-year-old. Oh well, mustn't grumble.'

'Elixir of youth?' Angie wrinkled her nose.

'Yes, I stumbled upon the formula a year or so after we last met. I was mixing some vodka—Oh... silly me, can't be giving away secrets. At least... not yet.' He smiled and winked.

Angie noticed his gold tooth. As a child she'd prayed his tooth would fall out one day so she could take it, imagining it would make her rich. A smile came to her lips at the recollection.

'Carrie can't remember coming here. Isn't that odd?'

'No, not odd at all. She was never here, only you, dear. Would you like a drink?' He stood up and walked towards the bar at the back of the room.

Angie hadn't noticed the bar before. It contained hundreds of colourful bottles.

'I wouldn't mind some of that elixir of youth,' she said, distractedly, still thinking about what Mr Silverfrost had said: *She was never here, only you.*

He laughed. 'All in good time.'

'Um, I really must go. I have to collect my children.'

'Ah yes, Ruby and Justine. Lovely girls.'

Angie's eyes widened. 'How... How...' She began to feel light-headed.

'Don't be alarmed. I can explain. But you have to suspend belief first.' His grey eyes stared into hers.

'Suspend belief?'

'Yes. It's not going to be easy for you to accept what I'm telling you. You have been so brainwashed into believing so many things.'

'I really have to go,' said Angie, suddenly struggling for air. 'I can't—'

'You're hyperventilating, that's all. Please breathe deeply and sit in my chair. I will try to explain.'

'But I have to go and collect the children.'

'They will be fine. Time is relative.'

Angie shook her head in confusion. 'Relative to what?'

'Let's just say that a minute to me is an hour to you and vice versa.'

'You're not making any sense.'

He rubbed his chin. 'See what I mean? It's hard to explain anything to someone who has been so conditioned to accept one way of looking at things. At one time people also believed the earth was flat, you know.'

'So you're telling me this is some kind of parallel universe?'

'If you want to think of it that way, yes. I exist and I don't exist, in the same way as you, my dear.'

'I'm confused,' said Angie, rubbing her forehead.

'That's perfectly understandable. Now, the reason I have summoned you to me—'

'Summoned me? Er... you didn't—'

Mr Silverfrost nodded. 'I did.'

'But... the reason I came here was because my sister had forgotten about the place and I wanted to see it again.'

'Yes, but why did you decide to come after all this time?'

'Because... Because...'

'Because I have a job for you.'

'You didn't "summon" me.'

'I called you, telepathically.'

Angie tried to rack her brain to remember why she started talking about the cottage with the purple door, but couldn't quite put her finger on it.

'I told you, you have to suspend belief, but here you go trying to find a reason for everything.' He raised his eyes skyward.

'Okay, well, why did you call me here?'

'The lady who works here needs your help.'

Angie looked around the room. 'The lady who works here?' She held her hands out, palms up, 'Where is she?'

'You have to be here at three o'clock on Wednesday, next week. Mrs Deborah Brown will be working here and your help will be required.'

'B-but I leave to collect my children at three. I won't make it in time if—'

'Make alternative arrangements. Be here. I cannot stress how important it is.'

'Why me? This makes no sense at all—'

Mr Silverfrost rubbed his chin. 'There you go.'

'Okay, okay, I'll suspend belief.' She rolled her eyes. 'I really must go.'

'Wait. You'll need this. Three drops on the tongue should do it. But make sure no one sees you.'

'What on earth? Oh, it doesn't matter.' She took the small vial, full of purple liquid, from his hands. The container was no larger than a perfume sample one might be given as a free gift in

14

a women's magazine. She turned to leave, but looked back over her shoulder at the old man. Then, shaking her head, she walked out of the door mumbling to herself, 'What was all *that* about?'

Back in the car, Angie inspected the vial and wondered what the purple liquid was. 'Three drops on the tongue,' she said out loud. Frowning, she realised she hadn't asked whether the liquid was for her or for "Deborah Brown". Putting the vial in her handbag, Angie jumped out of the car and walked back to the cottage.

The door was slightly ajar.

Once inside, she noticed to her horror that the room had taken on an altogether different appearance. Mr Silverfrost and his cat were nowhere to be seen. The walls seemed paler, and the bar that had once been there no longer existed. Everything was fading into a cloud-like substance. *What's going on? Where am I?* Feeling scared, and worried she might choke to death in the smoky air, Angie shuffled out of the door. *I'll have to ask him on Wednesday about the vial. Or I'll ask Deborah. What am I thinking? Am I really coming back here? Perhaps this is a dream. Yes, that's right, I fell asleep; an afternoon nap.*

On Sunday, Angie and her husband, Ivan, visited Carrie's house with their children.

When Ivan and Carrie's boyfriend, Jeff, were in the back garden playing with the children, Angie told her sister about seeing Mr Silverfrost at the old cottage. She hadn't even told Ivan, too afraid he would think she'd lost her mind. Even *she* was starting to doubt herself.

'Ang, I told you last week, I don't know Mr Snowfrost.'

'Silverfrost,' corrected Angie. She sighed and said, 'He actually told me you were never there, but—'

'Well, there you go,' said Carrie. 'I told you.'

'Yes... but in my memory you were there.' Angie gazed at the blue tiled floor.

'You were young at the time,' said Carrie, taking a biscuit from the plate on the table and dunking it in her tea. 'Perhaps your memory is a little confused. Maybe you used to go to the cottage with a friend.'

Angie wrinkled her brow and peered at Carrie. 'Hmm... I suppose that would explain why I thought someone else used to go with me; but Mr Silverfrost said it was *only* me.'

Shrugging, Carrie sipped her tea. 'Your tea's getting cold, sis.'

Angie pursed her lips and pulled her chair nearer to the table. She took hold of the teacup handle and ran her fingers along it, deep in thought. 'All of this has got me so confused.'

'Okay, look, let's go there together. I might see something that jogs my memory. It's possible I've just forgotten about it.' Carrie smiled at Angie, but then quickly looked away.

'You think I've gone nuts, don't you?'

'No.' Again Carrie could hardly meet her sister's eyes.

'Well, I wouldn't be surprised if you thought that. It's all so clear in my memory that you and I used to go and visit the cottage, but you say you don't remember, and I've been back there and met up with this "wizard" man. Perhaps I've been reading too many fantasy novels.'

Carrie giggled. 'Ivan and Jeff seem to be having fun out there with the kids,' she said, looking out of the patio doors. 'It'll take about half an hour for us to travel there and back. Let's go and visit this place. Maybe the old wizard'll be there and I can see what you're going on about.'

Angie brightened at this, a smile spreading across her lips, but then she recalled that the old man had not been there when she'd returned to ask about the vial. Was it all in her mind?

*

'It's along here. This one on the corner. Stop the car here...' Angie's voice trailed off.

'Where?' asked Carrie, agitatedly. 'I don't see a cottage with a purple door.'

'It was here. Is this Hobart Street?'

'Wait, let's drive to the end of the road where the road sign is,' said Carrie.

Angie's brain felt muddled. Suddenly her sense of direction was all askew. She'd found it without any trouble when she last came here. Number 1, Hobart Street, right on the corner.

'Yes, this is Hobart Street,' said Carrie. 'Which end of the street did you say? I can't see the numbering from here. No, wait, I can. That's number forty-five. Okay, we've come too far down the road. The cottage is on the corner, you say?'

Carrie's words flew over Angie's head as she peered out of the passenger window. *What's going on?* She began to feel foolish.

'Here's number one. But the door's green. Is this the right place?' asked Carrie.

'Do you think there're two Hobart Streets? No, how can that be? I came here last week. Wait, I recognise this tree with the pink blossom. The cottage was here.'

'Maybe he's painted the door.'

'What?'

'Well, it's possible.'

'But wait, this place has a sign outside: "Beatrice's..." Wait, what does that say?'

'Um... "Beatrice's Jewels". Ooh, let's take a look. I like handmade jewellery.' Carrie jumped out of the car.

Angie hesitantly followed her.

They walked up to the window. On display were pretty pieces of jewellery and trinket boxes, as well as various ornaments.

'I love these kinds of shops,' said Carrie. 'Let's go in!'

Angie followed, hardly able to believe her eyes.

As they walked in, a little bell jangled from above the entrance, announcing their arrival.

A middle-aged woman, with long brown hair, stood behind a counter at the far end of the room. She smiled brightly as they walked in. More handcrafted jewellery was displayed in the glass front of the counter, and behind it on the walls.

'Hello, I'm Debbie. Feel free to browse around, and let me know if I can help.' She beamed at them, revealing perfect white teeth.

Debbie? "Deborah Brown", "The lady who works here". Mr Silverfrost's words echoed in Angie's head.

Angie could not help staring at the woman. Luckily, Debbie seemed engrossed in a magazine article and didn't notice.

'Wow, these are nice,' said Carrie pointing to a pair of earrings displayed on the far wall.

Roused from her reverie by her sister's voice, Angie went to join her. 'Yes, they're lovely.'

'Twenty pounds. Hmm... Do you think that's expensive?'

'Um... I don't know.' Angie's mind was elsewhere and she wished they could leave.

'It's my birthday soon. I could get Jeff to buy them for me. What do you think?' Carrie held the silver dangly earrings next to her ear and smiled. 'Do they suit me?'

'Yes, they do,' said Angie, absent-mindedly.

'I'm going to buy them.' Carrie proceeded to take the earrings to the counter to pay for them.

Angie stood on the same spot, looking around her, but always finding her eyes resting on the woman, Debbie. The room was definitely the same one she had been in a few days ago, the only difference being the furniture—and the counter stood where the bar had been. The fireplace was in the same place, but without Mr Silverfrost's chair in front of it.

Angie peered over at the staircase and wondered whether Mr Silverfrost lived upstairs, and perhaps this was used as a shop on certain days of the week. That would make more sense. But would they really move all the furniture in and out so often? Unlikely. The most reasonable explanation would be that the shop had only started trading in the past couple of days. Perhaps Mr Silverfrost had sold the cottage, or was renting it out to make a bit of money.

Carrie chatted with the shopkeeper. 'Your jewellery is so beautiful. Do you make it yourself?'

'Some of it,' said Debbie. 'But others—like the ornaments and some of those necklaces over there—have been made by local artists. I like to help them sell their stuff. I started off quite small, but in the past couple of years business has really boomed; in fact,

I'm thinking of extending into the upstairs area, but I need to get the legal papers sorted to be able to do that. It involved a lot of red tape getting this converted to a shop. Used to be a residential property. Just off the high street is the perfect location for attracting customers who are out shopping in the area.' Debbie smiled her bright smile again.

'Well, I'll definitely be back!' said Carrie, proudly holding up the shiny red bag containing the newly purchased earrings.

'It's lovely to hear that.'

'Did you say you've been here for years?' asked Angie, thinking aloud.

Both Carrie and Debbie appeared almost startled by the question, perhaps not having expected her to speak as she'd been quiet for so long.

Debbie's smile soon found its way back to her face. 'Yes, I came here about five years ago. I love this area. I initially bought the place to live in—I live upstairs—but I just knew this would be the perfect site for my jewellery shop. The old man who lived here before left a lot of old furniture. His family said I could keep everything; that helped a lot with financing my business. I felt as though it was a parting gift from him, like he was backing my business enterprise. Yes, I know, it sounds crazy.' She rolled her eyes. 'I never met him, but I heard he liked to help people. Left a lot of money to local charities in his will. I like to think he watches over me, that's why the business is going so well.' She giggled.

'Ah, that's a sweet story,' said Carrie, glancing at Angie, eyebrows raised. 'What was the old man's name?'

'Mr Joseph Silverfrost. Lived to the ripe old age of ninety-five.'

Angie's mouth fell open. If he was dead, how had she seen him the week before? Goosebumps formed on her arms and she felt herself shiver.

Carrie gave Angie a knowing look.

Back in the car, Angie could hardly think straight. She kept replaying, in her head, the meeting with Mr Silverfrost and what he'd said.

'Carrie, what's happening to me?'

Carrie buckled the seatbelt and turned to face her. 'What do you mean?'

'I saw Mr Silverfrost last week. Right here, in this... shop. Well, it was a cottage then.'

Carrie remained silent as she put the car into gear and pulled away from the kerb.

'You think I'm imagining things, don't you?'

'No.' Carrie giggled, but her brow furrowed. 'You might be... I don't know. Maybe it was a dream.'

'Yes, a delusional dream in the daytime, when I was awake.' Angie sighed. 'Wait!' she said a bit too loudly, causing Carrie to nearly stall the car.

'What?'

'I was given a vial.'

'A what?'

'Mr Silverfrost, when he told me about Debbie, he gave me a vial. It's in my bag.' Angie picked up her handbag from the dashboard and fished inside. After emptying the entire contents onto her lap and rooting through them, she gave up the search. 'It was small,' she mumbled. 'It might have fallen out, or maybe the girls took it.' Sighing, she replaced all of her belongings into the bag, checking through them one last time. Feeling defeated, she put the handbag back onto the dashboard.

*

Wednesday morning came around quickly, almost as if time had sped up, racing towards that date. Angie had been tense all week, wanting to put what she'd seen down to a strange hallucination brought about by something she'd eaten that didn't agree with her, or working too hard, or not sleeping enough. Could the old memories have found their way into her mind when she'd spoken to Carrie about the cottage? Had she thought about it for too long, and consequently dreamt up the whole scenario of meeting with Mr Silverfrost?

Angie rubbed her eyes and sat up in bed. *Perhaps I did imagine it all.*

She glanced over at the rumpled empty space on the bed; Ivan had already left for work. What would he say if he knew about all of this? Angie silently laughed to herself. He'd think she'd finally gone completely mad. He often joked that she was bordering on delusional. Ivan wasn't a dreamer; he considered such attributes a weakness in a person. Sometimes Angie wondered how she'd ever ended up married to him.

She'd decided to go to the shop on Hobart Street at three o'clock. Arrangements were made for the children to be collected by one of the other mothers at Ruby and Justine's school. Annie, Claudette's mother, was happy to take the girls to her house for a play date after school.

Angie's stomach was in knots. She'd been unable to find the vial with the purple liquid, which made her think it more likely the meeting with Mr Silverfrost had never happened. Yet something compelled her to return to the shop. The driving force behind this decision was mostly made up of a need to prove she wasn't imagining it all. Occasionally a latent concern would surface: *Is this how dementia, Alzheimer's, or even schizophrenia starts?* Battling on, trying to ignore all the signs that she had concocted this whole thing in her head—a marvellous delusion leading her down a dark and confusing path—Angie kept telling herself everything would make sense if she saw it through to the end; there would be an explanation. The feeling that she was fooling herself remained a constant companion.

***

Pulling up in front of the jewellery shop on Hobart Street at ten minutes to three felt both unnerving and surreal. The last time Angie was here alone, this building had been the cottage with the purple door, but when she came with Carrie, the shop stood here, looking exactly as it did now. Her heart skipped a beat as a familiar thought assailed her: *Maybe I am losing my mind.*

Stepping out of the car, she tried to keep control of her

thoughts. *What am I doing here?* was the main one that kept bothering her, as she didn't have a definitive answer except that she'd been instructed to attend by an old man, who was—according to the latest evidence—well and truly dead.

She stopped outside the front of the shop and was about to turn on her heel when the thought "*Oh, this is stupid*" popped into her head for the tenth time that day; but then she saw Debbie exit the shop with something in her hand.

Debbie smiled at her, 'Hello. You were here the other day, weren't you?' she asked, squinting against the sun.

Her squint added an eerie quality to the question; Mr Silverfrost always squinted. The memory of the old man loomed large in Angie's head as she stared at the shopkeeper, mouth open. She nodded, a bit too enthusiastically, and said, 'Yes, yes, I came here with my sister.'

Debbie moved away from the front door. 'Please go in,' she said, with a flourish of her hand. 'Sorry for blocking the doorway, I'm just taking this letter to my neighbour; postman delivered it to the wrong address.'

Angie watched as the shopkeeper walked away. Her first thought was that she should get back into her car and scarper, but again something nagged her. *Huh, probably old Mr Silverfrost 'summoning' me again,* she mused.

She entered the shop. To her relief, the interior looked much the same as the last time she'd been there with Carrie. There was no sign of the old man and his cat.

Just as she was thanking her lucky stars, a cat wandered out from behind the counter. *Amber?* Angie took a step back and almost bumped into Debbie.

The cat rubbed against Angie's leg.

'Ah! I see you've met Marmalade? Don't worry,' said Debbie seeing Angie's wide eyes, 'she doesn't bite. She's very friendly.'

Angie relaxed slightly, pleased Debbie hadn't said its name was Amber, but she stared a bit too long at the cat because of the uncanny resemblance.

Debbie noticed. 'Do you have pets?' she asked, politely,

concern evident in her knitted brows.

'Um... no. Only goldfish,' said Angie, forcing her eyes away from the cat.

The cuckoo clock sounded, thankfully taking Debbie's attention away from Angie.

Three o'clock.

Just then, the door to the shop burst open and two men wearing balaclavas rushed in.

Debbie put her hands up in the air without being told to do so. 'Please take anything you want. Don't hurt us!' she said in a little-girl voice.

Angie froze on the spot. *The vial, the vial.* The words came to her mind and she scrabbled to find the opening of her handbag.

The two men were ransacking the shop by now, filling bin bags with jewellery, ornaments, and other items. Surprisingly, they hadn't appeared to notice Angie, even though she was standing near the entrance.

She found the vial at the top of her handbag, to her complete astonishment, and turned around before putting three drops of the purple fluid on her tongue, remembering Mr Silverfrost said no one should see her do it.

Turning back around, she saw Debbie had begun to cry.

Angie's eyes were drawn back to the men who were now looking directly at her, although it was hard to tell as their faces were more or less covered.

'Wh-what?' said one, seeming unable to continue.

'W-what? What shall we do, boss?' said the other, under his breath.

Both men remained rigid, as if they'd been frozen or turned to stone. Angie wondered whether that was the effect of the purple liquid.

'If we walk out slowly we should be okay,' replied the "boss".

'It looks like some kind of guard dog.'

'Leave the stuff here,' said the boss.

They both lowered the bin bags they were carrying and placed them on the floor.

'Right, well, you go first... slowly,' ordered the boss.

'I'm not going first,' said the other, sounding like a little boy.

Debbie lowered her arms. 'Are you going to leave my shop, or am I going to have to call the police?' she asked, appearing to have regained her confidence.

The two men turned towards Debbie and then looked back at Angie.

Debbie huffed, and picked up the telephone on her counter.

Minutes later, sirens were heard.

The two men were still standing in the same place, and Debbie was still behind the counter when the police arrived. Angie stayed just beside the entrance, where she had been from the start.

After the police had asked Debbie a few questions, the men were cautioned and led away from the scene.

'But we didn't take anything,' protested the one referred to as "boss".

When the men had gone, Debbie ran out from behind the counter and picked up the cat who was settling down to sleep. 'Good old Marmalade, hey?' she said cuddling the cat who squirmed and did its utmost to get away.

Angie's eyes widened. 'You mean they were afraid of the cat?'

'Yeah, weird, huh? What are the chances of two burglars being scared of this little cutie?' Debbie giggled, wiping a stray tear from her cheek as she released the cat from her hold.

'But... they said something about a guard dog,' said Angie, frowning and remembering the way the two men had been staring directly at her the whole time.

'I know!' Debbie laughed. 'Fancy that. I had no idea people could be so scared of cats.'

Debbie twisted around and looked at the bin bags on the floor. 'Oh, no.' She sighed, 'how am I going to get all this sorted out? I'll have to close the shop for today. I hope nothing's broken.'

'I'll help you,' said Angie, thinking that perhaps this was the "help" Mr Silverfrost had been referring to.

*

The news item was tucked away at the bottom of the right-hand side of page twelve of the local paper a few days later. Neither Debbie nor Angie saw it.

The story read:

Silly news item of the week: *Two men were arrested on Wednesday afternoon after attempting to raid a local jeweller's shop. The men reportedly planned to get away with hundreds of pounds worth of handmade jewellery and other decorative items, packing them into black bin bags. They were stopped in their tracks when the owner of the shop called the police.*

The men were apparently too scared to leave the premises due to a large dog guarding the entrance. One of the burglars protested to the police who arrested him, stating that people should not be allowed to own such large dogs. By the description, the dog that scared the men may have been of the Newfoundland breed which has been known to grow to over six feet from nose to tail.

However, the breed does not specifically fall under the Dangerous Dogs Act, and the animal had not acted aggressively; the size of the dog had been the issue. A local solicitor has told us it's unusual for the owners of a placid dog to be taken to court, and although size could be a factor in a judge's determination as to whether a dog is dangerous or not, there should be some aggression shown by the animal if it is to be classified as "dangerous".

To add further strangeness to this story, when the police questioned the owner about her "dog", she confirmed she only owns a cat—a very small cat. This has led police to question whether the men had been partaking of a hallucinatory drug before trying to rob the jeweller's shop. There were no other witnesses.

Far Away In Time - Part II

Angie drove along the familiar road, gripping the steering wheel tightly, her jaw clenched.

Ever since the day at the jewellery shop, she had been unable to relax. The meeting with Mr Silverfrost and then the subsequent attempted burglary hovered in her mind like a dream, or a reflection that she tried to get a closer grip of, but that would slip away at the last moment.

None of it made sense.

A whole calendar month had gone by since she was last here. She'd spoken to no one about it, afraid of being ridiculed. There was only that one night, a couple of weeks ago, when Ruby asked her to read a bedtime story. Angie reached over to the bookshelf and picked out *The Velveteen Rabbit*, one of Ruby's favourites, but Ruby groaned and said: 'No, Mummy, I want you to make up a story. I like your made-up stories.'

Angie proceeded to tell her the story of an old wizard who lived in a corner shop and could only be seen by two little girls. His magical potions saved the day when two evil burglars tried to steal his precious jewels. Angie felt better after telling the story, like a burden had been lifted, even though to Ruby it was just a fantastical tale that she'd probably forget in a couple of days. By the time Angie got to the part where the burglars entered the shop, Ruby was asleep, but Angie carried on telling the story, in a whisper, breaking through the silence in the dark room as if she were confessing a sin.

*

Holding her breath, Angie approached the turning into Hobart Street. On her last visit, there'd been the attempted burglary at the jewellery shop, but when she'd visited on her own before that, the door was the old purple one she'd known from her youth, and old Mr Silverfrost had been there to greet her. Which would she encounter this time?

She had spent many hours in the past few weeks deliberating over whether it was all in her imagination; like the time she'd taken out one of her earrings and then tried to remove the other one, but it wasn't there. She'd thought it must have fallen off, and retraced her footsteps through her house, finally giving up the search. Later, she found the earring on her ear. It had been there all along.

Wondering whether she might be losing her mind became a common thought process for Angie in the weeks following the attempted burglary at "Beatrice's Jewels". The vial, which she was sure she'd put into her handbag after applying the three drops to her tongue, had vanished. Despite emptying the contents of her handbag on more than one occasion, and going through them one by one, the whereabouts of the glass tube remained a mystery.

Angie pulled up outside number 1, Hobart Street, and to her astonishment the purple door came into sight. Her eyes widened and she forced herself to close and open them again. She even pinched herself, accidentally drawing a little blood with the sharp edge of her nail. After licking the wound, she turned her head slowly towards the old purple door. No sign of the jewellery shop.

Taking a deep breath, Angie got out of her car almost forgetting to close and lock the door behind her.

Curious, she opened her handbag. Lo and behold, the first

27

thing she saw was the vial; still full of the purple liquid. Her heart skipped a beat and she looked around, trying to work out if anything else had changed. Had she unwittingly passed through a portal to another world? Or could this be an unexplained phenomenon, like the Bermuda Triangle? But everything else seemed the same. *Except...* One notable difference struck her: she was completely alone, as if the last person on earth. Racking her brain, she tried to remember whether that had been the case before.

Tumultuous thoughts battling for her attention, Angie walked straight into the cottage, not even bothering to knock, knowing that wouldn't be necessary.

'There you go,' said Mr Silverfrost as soon as she entered the room, before even saying hello, 'trying to make sense of everything again.'

Angie peered at him and blinked, in an attempt to make him disappear, or to make herself wake up, or to shake whatever this madness was. 'Um... hello... er... what?'

'Nice to see you again, Angie.' He wore a wide grin. 'You did a grand job helping to deter those would-be intruders.'

She shook her head and frowned. 'I really don't know what you mean.'

Mr Silverfrost touched his chin and sighed. 'Let me explain.' He gestured for her to take a seat.

Behind her, she saw a white leather armchair, which had materialised as if by magic. She lowered herself, tentatively, into the chair, worried in case it might somehow vanish, or transport her to another place.

Mr Silverfrost pressed a switch on the top of the mantelpiece. The wall above the fireplace transformed into a widescreen cinematic television, and pictures began flickering on the screen as if from an old projector. Slowly the faded images came into focus.

Angie's mouth fell open when she saw herself on the screen, large as life, at the entrance to the jewellery shop, Debbie behind the counter.

'Wa-wait. Is this CCTV footage?'

'No,' said Mr Silverfrost. 'This is a cerebral reconstruction of events.'

'A cerebr—what? But that's me.'

'Of course it is,' said the old man. 'There were no cameras on the actual day, but all of this was stored in your memory. I'm merely helping you to see events as they really happened, not as you perceived them.'

'I don't understand,' said Angie.

'If you keep frowning like that it'll stick, you know,' said Mr Silverfrost. 'Do you want such deep wrinkles? Please try to relax.'

Angie sighed. 'Couldn't I have some of your elixir of youth?' she asked, stretching her brow consciously in an effort to rid herself of the frown that had become a permanent fixture ever since she'd walked into the room.

The old man guffawed. 'All in good time,' he said.

She watched as events unfolded on the screen and saw herself turn around. *That was when I put the three drops of the purple liquid on my tongue*, she recalled.

The burglars were throwing items from the shop into black bin bags.

Debbie stood frozen in fear, wide-eyed.

Staring at the screen, Angie looked from herself to Debbie and back again. She let out a gasp when she saw a creature. Was it some kind of bear? No, a dog: a very large dog. In the "film footage", the animal stood where she had originally been standing. The dog appeared to be over six feet tall.

'Surprised?' quizzed Mr Silverfrost, raising an eyebrow.

Angie pointed at the image on the wall and then turned towards the old wizard.

Mr Silverfrost clicked the button on the mantelpiece and the old framed painting of a battle scene was restored to the wall, replacing the widescreen television.

'What's going on?' she managed to say. 'Th-this is all in my head.' She held her forehead and stood up.

'Not at all,' said Mr Silverfrost.

'When I came here before, this was a shop, now it's a... a... I don't know—'

'You are experiencing an alternative reality.'

'What? What do you mean?' Her frown returned.

'My reality is different to your reality. This is mine.'

'How—'

'Suffice to say, the liquid in the vial aids the transition.'

Angie rummaged through her bag and took out the vial.

'Our friends—the burglars—saw another reality, which reflected their inner fears. That's why they were unable to leave the shop,' explained Mr Silverfrost.

'They saw that dog?'

'Yes, exactly.'

'But... Debbie didn't.'

'Debbie had no reason to see another reality.'

'Okay, so wait, Debbie is real?'

'Why, of course.'

'Well.' Angie raised her eyebrows. 'Where is she?'

'She's here.'

'But—'

'Don't try to understand. Let's just say you needed to see me today, so that I could explain what happened. Next time you come here, I won't be here.'

A sudden sense of loss inexplicably gripped Angie. 'So that means I'll never see you again?'

'That isn't what I said.'

'Okay, but how come I saw this reality if I didn't take any liquid from the vial? And how come I can see the vial now? I was looking for—'

'There is so much you do not know, and much for you to learn.'

'So what would happen if I put three drops on my tongue now?'

The old man squinted and shrugged.

Angie frowned again and then immediately raised her eyebrows, self-consciously, to rid herself of the frown. She sighed and unsecured the lid. Holding the vial in position, she felt the three drops of liquid fall onto her tongue, then watched as the world spun around her as if she'd been thrown into a washing machine cycle, the colours swirling in a clockwise direction.

When the whirling stopped, she found herself in the jewellery shop. No sign of Mr Silverfrost, no vial in her hand.

Debbie smiled at her from behind the counter. 'Angie! So lovely to see you again.'

Echoes Of Her Dreams

Looking out of the window, as she sipped her tea, Charlene noticed a seagull hovering in the cloud-filled sky, noisily making its presence known. *Seagulls are perpetually angry*, she mused. The bird continued to screech, sounded like it was screaming. *Seagulls are the avian equivalent of the football hooligan*; a smile curled the edges of her lips as the thought entered her mind.

Just then, a crow landed on the flat roof across the street. The majestic-looking bird sat and preened its feathers for a short moment and then took off again.

Charlene sighed as the phone in her office began to ring for the fiftieth time that morning. *Oh, to be a bird*.

Catching sight of the coaster on the desk in front of her, its photo depicting a coastline and perfect crystal-clear sea, she felt a yearning to escape into the idyllic seascape. Unable to ignore the persistent ringing of the phone, she placed her cup of tea onto the coaster, reluctantly obscuring the picture, and begrudgingly answered the call.

Later that evening, Charlene was preparing dinner for her family; husband, Zac, and son, Lion. Yes, *Lion*. Zac chose the name. He said he wanted a "strong" and "manly" name for their son. They were only teenagers when Lion was born, and when Zac's dad said, 'It's a stupid idea to name a child after a big cat,' that was all the encouragement Zac needed to go ahead, even though Charlene secretly hated the name. She never referred to him as Lion, but preferred to call him Li, for short (pronounced *lie*). Consequently, hardly any of her friends knew what his full name was. One of her friends made the mistake of referring to him as Lionel when he was a toddler: 'Oh, Lionel's grown so much since the last time I saw him!' Charlene merely smiled and didn't bother correcting her.

The lottery was on television as they sat around the table eating the lamb chops and chips she had prepared. Charlene silently prayed she would win the jackpot and finally get a chance to travel and do all the things she yearned to do.

Li was leaving home in less than a month, due to start university. Part of her wanted to keep him locked up in his room, but another part of her knew the time had come for him to leave the nest. An element of fear mixed with excitement stirred within her as she contemplated the end of an era and a new beginning: she'd made up her mind to divorce Zac as soon as Li left for university.

Rightly or wrongly, Charlene blamed Zac for clipping her wings. On finding out she was pregnant with Li, an angry weed sprouted in her head. Her thoughts fertilized the weed over the years. Every single time anything happened to stop her from chasing her dreams, she would complain to Zac.

Lately, his most common response was, 'You're a mother of an intelligent, strong, and decent young man, and you've got a job. Look at our friends; what have they achieved in their lives? I think we've done all right, don't you? You should be grateful for what you've got. Lots of people would kill to be in your shoes.'

His next sentence was usually a variation of, 'Is the dinner ready yet?' or 'Get me a cup of tea, please, love.'

Charlene couldn't put her finger on it, but knew there must be so much more to life. She felt selfish and guilty, aware she had been almost counting time for the past eighteen years, waiting for

Li to start his own life so she could get on with hers.

'Don't give me that,' Zac would say, whenever she said she could have accomplished great things if they hadn't had Li when they were so young. 'If you really wanted to do something, you'd have done it, Li or no Li, and whether or not you were married to me. Face it, Charlie. Lots of women juggle children with careers and other stuff.'

When Zac would say such things, Charlene often wondered if he was right. Had she been using Li as an excuse for not doing what she wanted to?

Upon discovering she was pregnant with Li, Charlene had withdrawn from the A-Level course she'd enrolled in, thinking it wouldn't be possible to study *and* have a baby.

'Becoming a mother is a great responsibility, Charlie,' her own mother told her. 'You need to give the baby all your attention. There's really no need for you to study, anyway, is there, darling? Zac's such a lovely boy and he's got a job. He can support you and the little one.'

Sometimes, Charlene resented the way her parents stood behind her decision to quit her A-Levels. Couldn't they have helped out with the baby so she could get some qualifications? The sense of resentment intensified as the weeks and months turned into years and she stayed at home looking after Li, feeling unhappy and as if she was missing out on a whole world happening outside her window. Everyone else seemed to be living their lives, while she remained stuck in some time warp where nothing ever changed.

She turned down invites from her friends for nights out.

'You're a mum now, you can't go gallivanting around at all hours,' Zac opined on many occasions, often followed by, 'I'm going down the pub for a while, see you later.'

The chasm of disillusionment grew and grew until Charlene felt afraid she would disappear inside.

A few years later, Melissa, Charlene's younger sister, became pregnant at the age of sixteen and wasn't sure who the father of her child was. She didn't want to have an abortion, though, and begged Charlene to help her with the baby.

'But now Li is about to start school I wanted to maybe take a course at college,' said Charlene. 'You know how much I've always wanted to study English Literature or Art, and travel someday. I've been stuck indoors with Li for so long. I want to spread my wings. Now's the time for me to be looking at what I want to do.'

'Oh, sis, those are dreams,' said Melissa. 'Life's hard these days. People have to work to survive. You're lucky because you've got Zac to support you. What've I got?' Melissa twisted a brown lock of hair around her finger as she spoke, eyes down, intermittently peeking up from beneath her eyelashes briefly enough for Charlene to see tears threatening to fall.

Charlene frowned as she gazed at her younger sister. She didn't want Melissa to end up feeling as depressed as herself, sometimes contemplating ending it all.

So Charlene became the full-time carer for her nephew, baby Tiger (yes, it seems the big cat name was popular in the family). Her own "dreams" would have to wait.

'I'm so grateful, sis. You have no idea how much you're doing for me. I'll repay you one day,' gushed Melissa. 'I'm going to finish college and get a really good job, then we'll go travelling, like you've dreamed of doing, just me and you.'

'What about the kids?' asked Charlene, raising her eyebrows.

'They'll have grown up by then.' Melissa smiled sweetly.

Melissa did finish college, but then decided she wanted to go to university. Once again, she begged Charlene to look after Tiger. Charlene had grown fond of the boy by then, and agreed to help out.

When Melissa finished university she did find a good job, working in the city; but that meant Charlene had to carry on caring for Tiger while Melissa worked full-time.

Eventually, Melissa met a man who whisked her and Tiger away to start a new life in Brighton. Charlene hardly ever saw her sister or nephew for the next few years, and nowadays Christmas was the only time their paths crossed.

When Melissa left, taking Tiger with her, Li was about ten years old. Having never worked before, Charlene felt so out of her depth seeking employment. She lacked confidence, having spent most of the past decade raising the two boys and not doing much else.

When she first mentioned to Zac that she wanted to go to college, he laughed and told her, 'We can't afford to have you studying. This is the real world, Charlie!' He said it was "about time" she started working and contributing to the household finances.

'Excuse me?' she said, eyes narrowed, feeling insulted by his comment, 'I've been looking after your son for the past ten years, so don't you dare tell me I haven't been contributing!'

'*My* son? He's always *my* son, not yours, when you wanna try and make out I'm wrong about something, isn't he?' Zac huffed. 'I'll have you know, if it wasn't for you spending so much time babysitting your sister's illegitimate son, we'd be much better off. She never even paid you, did she?'

'Uh... she's my sister, she didn't have to pay me.' Charlene shook her head.

'She might be your sister, but she's not mine,' he said, gruffly, pointing an accusatory finger at her. 'And she took the piss if you ask me, expecting you to bring up her sprog while she went around acting like a single woman, dating all sorts of men. You should have stood up to her.'

Charlene's eyes widened. 'I wanted to help with Tiger. He's my nephew. And Mel has found a nice man. Paul's a gentleman. She wasn't picking up random men. A friend introduced her to Paul, actually. Mel was badly burned by Tiger's father, she wasn't really keen on dating anyone.'

Zac started laughing. 'Oh my God, can you hear yourself? Have you forgotten what a slut your little sister was? She doesn't even know who Tiger's father is. She must've slept with at least two boys at her school by the age of sixteen for that to be the case.'

'She wasn't a slut. Just a typical teenager.'

'And who names their son "Tiger", for God's sake?' Zac spluttered.

'Um... our son is called Lion thanks to you, remember?'

Zac stood up and pushed past her. 'I'm going to the pub. Don't wait up.'

Without Zac's backing, Charlene couldn't afford to study, so she signed on at the local Jobcentre and found a few temping appointments. After six months she found a job as an office clerk at the local council. Eight years later she was still there. She came and went each day, dissatisfied, but forever being told she should be grateful for what she had.

'There's a recession,' Zac would keenly remind her every time she so much as mentioned her desire to try looking for another job.

The years drifted by, and when she heard Li talk about his hopes for the future she would hear the echoes of her own dreams coming back to her as if from some faraway land calling her home. *Not long now; Li will be going to uni, and I'll leave Zac. Then my life will start.*

Her lottery numbers didn't come up that night, and after washing the dinner plates she was screwing up the pink slip of paper when Li entered the kitchen.

'Hi, Mum, can I talk to you about something?'

'Of course. What's up, love? Getting last minute nerves about starting uni?' she asked, noticing his shifty demeanour.

'No,' he said, not meeting her eyes. He looked up coyly and smiled briefly. Then, sighing, he took a seat next to the kitchen table.

Charlene threw the lottery ticket into the bin, and instinctively sat beside Li. Reaching out and rubbing the top of his arm, she sensed a sadness she couldn't really understand. She had thought he was overjoyed to be starting university; he'd talked about nothing else for the past few weeks.

'I have some news,' he said.

She noticed a twinkle in his eye then, but he still appeared reticent, as if afraid to say whatever he wanted to tell her.

Eyes down, she placed both hands on her lap, smoothing her apron. 'What is it?'

'Candy's pregnant.'

Candy was Li's girlfriend.

Charlene put a hand over her mouth. The news came as a surprise; a pleasant one. She smiled, but noticed Li seemed unable to meet her eyes. 'That's lovely news. But is there something you're not telling me? You don't seem happy about it...'

'I am—'

'Oh, I know: Candy won't be able to go to uni with you now, will she?' Charlene nodded, understanding. 'Poor Candy,' she said, thinking aloud. 'I bet she'll be upset.' She recalled how she'd shelved her own studies on finding out she was pregnant. Funny how history had a way of repeating itself.

'No... No, Mum, you've misunderstood.' Li glanced at her bashfully. 'I... I was going to ask you if you'd look after the baby while we're at uni. Candy'll still be able to do the course. The university has agreed. But when the baby's born—it's due in about six months—we'll need someone to help out. I can't think of anyone better than you, Mum,' he said, his blue eyes pleading.

Charlene's own eyes widened. 'M-m-me?'

'Yes, Mum.' Li became animated as he went on to explain that he and Candy had discussed everything and decided they wanted her to mind the baby for them.

Charlene felt her dreams once again drifting away; once again put on hold. Her plans to divorce Zac; the money she'd been secretly squirrelling away into a separate bank account; the online surfing she'd done, looking for places she could get away to; all the travel she had planned...

'Mum?'

Li's voice disturbed her reverie. She snapped back to the present. 'Yes, of course. I would be delighted.' She stood up and wiped some crumbs off her apron. As she glanced out of the window, a sparrow twisted its head towards her and then took off, flying away into the vast blue sky.

A Sign

Pulling at the worn-out carpet, wanting to make a start on removing it before the fitters arrived, Grace noticed a crack in one of the wooden floorboards. She applied a bit of pressure with her hand and the board broke in two. A frown settled on her brow. Finally moving into her own house after years of living in other people's homes was something she'd been looking forward to. She felt deflated now, anxious about the cost of repairing the floorboard.

The hideous lime-green carpet was an eyesore, and she'd intended to replace it as soon as she moved in. The new carpet was being delivered later that day.

'Hmm... How am I going to get this fixed before the fitters come?' she grumbled to herself, falling into a sulk.

Grace replaced the broken board as best she could, wincing when a splinter got caught in her finger. Gritting her teeth, she pulled at the sliver of wood lodged in her forefinger, relieved when it came out quite easily, glad she wouldn't have to search through the jumble of unpacked belongings to find her tweezers.

Dusting off her hands, and standing up, she surveyed the ugly green carpet, wondering for the fiftieth time why anyone would have chosen it for their house; at best, the colour was migraine-inducing. Walking over to the mantelpiece, she picked up her mobile phone.

'Hi,' she said on hearing her brother's voice. 'Listen, do you know anything about fixing broken floorboards?'

Two hours later, the floorboard was as good as new, just in

time for the new carpet to be laid; a gorgeous deep burgundy shade that reminded her of red wine.

*

Grace sat staring at the jewellery box sitting on the table in front of her. The old-fashioned box had silver rims, with an inlaid tortoiseshell design, and reminded her of one of those boxes she had seen on television programmes about antiques. Picking it up, she fiddled with the catch again.

She'd found the jewellery box while waiting for her brother to arrive to fix the broken floorboard. She had been trying to work out whether it would have to be replaced or if it could be mended. As she lifted up the floorboard, a ray of sun reflected off the silver edge and she'd noticed the jewellery box, partially obscured by a piece of cardboard. She wondered how long it had lain undiscovered. Just then, the doorbell rang, and she felt the need to hide the pretty box, wanting to be the first person to see what treasure it held.

Grace ran into the kitchen and hid the little box in one of the cupboards. The discovery remained in her mind all the time her brother was fixing the floorboard, and when the carpet fitters came. She found herself willing them to finish their tasks quickly and leave, so she could retrieve the ornate box and take a peek inside.

*

Frustration etched creases in her forehead as she sat holding the jewellery box, unable to fathom a way to open it. She hadn't wanted to ask for help; that would spoil everything. Her amazing discovery—because she had by now convinced herself it was an amazing discovery—could not be touched by anyone. *There must be something valuable inside*, she reasoned, *otherwise, why bother hiding it under the floorboard?*

Sighing, she decided to put the box back into the kitchen cupboard until she could think of a way to open it.

41

Grace went into the bedroom and began to unpack her belongings, placing her clothes in the fitted wardrobe. She used a footstool to access the top inner shelf of the tall wardrobe, so she could tidy away her towels.

As she reached into the top shelf, her hand scraped against a nail sticking out of the side. Flinching, she inspected the sharp gash on her hand and began to worry in case the nail was rusty. Her imagination ran wild at the slightest injury. Shaking the negative thoughts from her mind, she went back downstairs to the kitchen and found a packet of antiseptic wipes.

Whilst looking for a packet of plasters in one of the kitchen cupboards, she noticed a rectangular object protruding over the back of the shelf. On further inspection, it appeared to be built into the back wall. *It's probably an old plug socket that's been covered up.* Shrugging, she closed the door.

After cleaning her scratch and securing the plaster on her hand, Grace opened the cupboard door to replace the packet of plasters. Noticing the strange object again, she stretched her hand towards the back of the shelf and tugged at it; there was a slight movement. With one final pull, a metallic cover came away. Behind the cover was nothing but a dent in the concrete wall.

Just then, her eye rested on something shiny on the shelf, immediately below where the cover had been. *It must have fallen out... must have been concealed there for years.* Exhilaration coursed through her veins. Was it some kind of jewel, or a valuable coin? Holding her breath, Grace picked up the shiny object. Her brow furrowed when she saw it was a small metal key. 'Not an antique then,' she mumbled to herself, her high spirits waning.

About to throw the key back into the cupboard, she remembered the jewellery box. Once again, her level of excitement bubbled upwards. Could this be the key that fit the box? *Wow! There must be something special in that box if the owner went to such lengths to hide the key!* She could hardly contain her eagerness, feeling like a five-year-old playing a treasure hunt game.

Leaning over, she opened the cupboard below the kitchen worktop, retrieved the jewellery box, and gently placed it on the kitchen table as if it were fragile. Her hand shook slightly, with nervous anticipation, as she tried opening the decorative box with the little key. However, her efforts were in vain; the key did not fit the lock.

Refusing to be beaten, she sat down to position herself closer to the box, and tried again. At one point the key entered the lock, but wouldn't turn. *The lock might be rusted with age.* Grace stared at the beautiful jewellery box, narrowing her eyes, as if it were an adversary.

Standing up, she grabbed the box, no longer treating it with any reverence, minded to use a hammer to finally end her torment and find out what it contained. Instead, she practically threw the jewellery box back into the kitchen cupboard.

The little silver key, along with the strange metal cover that had concealed it, remained discarded on the kitchen table as she rolled her eyes and walked back upstairs wondering why on earth someone would go to so much trouble to hide a key that meant nothing to anyone.

Later that evening, Grace sat in the living room watching television. Her eye kept being drawn to the painting on the wall above the television set; an old oil painting. The ocean scene with crashing waves, depicted in the painting, was not to her taste. It didn't help that the colours were drab, having faded over time.

When the programme she'd been watching came to an end, she decided to replace the painting with one of her own.

Rummaging through the removal boxes, she found the painting she was looking for: a New York street scene. A smile came to her lips as she gazed at it, memories of her holiday flashing through her mind. She'd been staying in Times Square on a trip to New York and had spotted a vendor selling art by the side of the busy street. This artwork seemed to encapsulate all she loved about the city; a vibrant scene, showing Times Square in all its glory: bright lights, people, yellow taxi cabs, theatre hoardings.

That'll cheer the place up until I can decorate, she thought to herself, frowning at the browny-beige wallpaper that looked as though it could have been the original wallpaper from when the house was built back in the early part of the twentieth century.

Grace sat the New York scene painting by the side of the television unit and, reaching up, took down the old painting, sneezing as loose dust particles were dispersed. She raised an eyebrow on seeing the light beige rectangle on the wall where the original painting had lived. She quite liked the colour of the wallpaper beneath; much better than the dull brown it had become over the years. She ran a hand over the paper and noticed it was actually embossed with small lines, something that couldn't really be seen on the faded and aged wallpaper in the rest of the room. It made her wonder just how long the painting had hung there. Years? Decades?

Moving her hand along the wall, she could feel something. *What is that?* It didn't feel like part of the wall. Knowing she would be redecorating soon, she began to peel off a bit of the wallpaper, eager to discover what lay beneath. There was something metallic underneath it, not plaster or brick as she'd expected to find. Then, with a final tug on the wallpaper, all was revealed: it was a safe.

The key she'd left on the kitchen table fit the safe perfectly. As the lock clicked open she felt a great sense of excited anticipation, as if she were about to uncover an ancient mystery.

Her face fell when she pulled back the door, only to find the recess empty. Lots of dust was emitted as the wallpaper pulled away from the wall to reveal the gaping hole. *I hope there isn't any asbestos in these walls.* As the thought occurred to her that there was every possibility there might be, she decided it would be best to shut the safe door. About to step down from the footstool, she noticed something glinting on the base of the safe.

Another key? Her thoughts immediately went to the jewellery box.

The key fit the lock of the ornate box perfectly, twisting with an ease as if it had been waiting for one hundred years to find the place it belonged.

Euphoria causing her stomach to somersault, Grace held

her breath and lifted the lid of the old jewellery box. On seeing its contents, a disappointed sigh left her lips. No treasure. Just a piece of paper folded in two, and another key—this one even smaller than the one she'd used to open the box. Frowning, she unfolded the paper, which almost crumbled between her fingers, and read: *"Tony, A note for you! I told you I'd get a message to you somehow. I'll always love you, Sarah x"*

Grace turned the piece of paper over, but the back was blank. She inspected the box to see if there was anything else—a hidden panel perhaps—but she found nothing more.

As she twisted the tiny key between her fingers, she wondered who Tony and Sarah were, how many years this letter and key were under the floorboard, and why the key to the jewellery box was in the safe.

Reluctantly, she put the key and letter back into the jewellery box and stored it in the kitchen cupboard again, resigning herself to the fact that her questions would probably remain unanswered.

*

A few days later, Grace had just arrived home from work and was about to open her front door, when she heard a voice behind her.

'You settling in okay?' asked the gruff-sounding man's voice.

Turning around, Grace caught sight of a large man who bore a wide grin. He stood at the gate to her neighbour's house, but she hadn't seen him before, as far as she could recall. An old woman lived next door. Grace hadn't found time to introduce herself properly to the woman and wasn't entirely sure whether anyone else lived in the house with her.

'I'm Antoinette's son,' said the man, by way of explanation, faced with Grace's blank stare. He opened the gate and walked towards the neighbour's front door.

'Antoinette?' Grace echoed.

'Yes.' The man pointed to the old woman's house. 'I'm guessing you haven't met my mum yet? She's the woman who lives here. I'm visiting. She loves visitors; you should get to know her. She loves to chat. She's lived in this street for a hundred years.' He chuckled. 'She could fill you in on all the goings-on here since the year dot. I assumed you'd met her already. She's told me all about you and your cat.'

He walked to the door of the house and put a key in the lock. 'Well,' he said over his shoulder, 'it was nice meeting you. I'm sure we'll be seeing a lot of each other. Er... I'm John, by the way.'

'Um... Grace. Nice to meet you too,' she said.

He nodded and smiled before disappearing into the house.

News travels fast around here, she thought, confused as to how the old woman, Antoinette, knew about her cat. She'd only brought him home from the rescue shelter the day before. *Maybe she was peeking through her curtains.*

Back in the house, preparing dinner, Grace suddenly had a thought: if Antoinette had lived in this street for decades, she might have known the people who lived here before—years before. Sarah... Tony. It would be worth asking. It could solve the mystery of the letter in the jewellery box, and the little key.

*

The next day, after work, Grace knocked on Antoinette's door.

After a couple of minutes, and just when Grace was about to walk away, the door slowly creaked open and the old woman greeted her with a smile.

'Hello, Grace. Lovely to meet you at last,' she said in a croaky voice, similar in tone to that of the wicked witch from *The Wizard of Oz.*

'How did you know my name?' Grace gulped.

'You met my son yesterday, introduced yourself.'

Thoughts of the man she'd met outside the house the day before sprang to Grace's mind. 'Oh yes, of course.'

'I knew all about you before, though,' continued Antoinette, 'because I asked my neighbour, Geraldine, when she was selling the house. She was a good friend of mine. Told me all about you before she moved out. I hope we can be friends too.' The old woman stepped aside. Pointing into the dimly lit hallway, she continued, 'Would you like to come in for a cup of tea? You look tired. Been working all day? You youngsters need to learn to relax more, take time to dream.'

Grace's eyes were drawn to the chandelier that lit the hallway. The whole ambience was reminiscent of an old horror movie. She expected a ghoul or zombie to jump out from somewhere. Shaking away her irrational thoughts, she replied: 'Um... I can come for tea tomorrow. I'm not working then. I just wanted to introduce myself. Sorry I haven't been over before. I've been busy unpacking.'

'Just as I said, young people don't know how to relax anymore.' Antoinette turned to face her again. 'Let's say four o'clock tomorrow. I'll bake some biscuits.'

'No need to go to any bother—'

'Oh, it's a pleasure. I love the smell of home-made cakes.'

Antoinette's voice conjured up thoughts of evil stepmothers in fairy tales, and Grace worried the biscuits might be poisoned and she would fall asleep for a hundred years. She struggled to rid her mind of the strange thoughts that overwhelmed her in this woman's presence. 'Um... yes, tomorrow at four,' she said, forcing a smile.

Once back in her house, Grace felt a rush of relief. 'Oh, my God,' she said aloud to herself, 'what am I letting myself in for?'

*

At 4 p.m., the following day, Grace knocked on Antoinette's front door.

When the old woman let her in, Grace noticed that the inside of the house appeared much brighter in the daylight without the dim lighting from the chandelier casting gloomy shadows. She felt silly for fearing visiting the place.

She followed Antoinette along the hallway, the smell of freshly baked muffins wafting through the house. The house was identical in size and shape to her own, and also decorated in a

47

similar fashion, Grace noted. It had the same browny-beige wallpaper in the living room. However, this house had a warmer, more lived-in feel. The carpet was a beautiful shade of green that brought to mind palm leaves. The velvet curtains matched it perfectly.

'Please make yourself at home, dear,' said Antoinette pointing to a lovely soft, cream-coloured, leather sofa.

Even the old woman's voice didn't sound as witchy as the evening before. The darkness of the evening had somehow tricked Grace's mind. The house was very welcoming.

Grace looked at the coffee table and saw a teapot with a rose-coloured tea cosy sitting on a gleaming silver tray. Beside it sat a cake plate full of the delicious-smelling muffins. The pretty doily underneath completed the home-made and house-proud aura.

Grace smiled and sat down on the sofa. It was surprisingly comfortable; her whole body relaxed as she took a seat. 'Lovely, comfy sofa,' she said speaking her thoughts.

'Yes, my Johnny bought it for me last year. I have arthritis; need something comfy. It was very expensive. I told him off for spending so much money, but he wanted me to have it: "Nothing but the best for my mum," he said to me. I'm so proud of him. Just wish I'd had more children. I married late. I was forty-seven when I had my Johnny, you know. Unheard of in those days. Of course, nowadays all the career women are putting off starting a family. I say, start when you're young. I would have been glad to have ten of Johnny. He's a diamond.' Antoinette walked over to the other side of the sofa and sat down. 'Are you single?' she asked.

'Yes,' said Grace.

'My son is single too. He's such a good man. Lived with his wife for ten years, then she left him for another man. His children, Jemima and Martha, are so beautiful. Sometimes he brings them to visit. His youngest, Martha, reminds me so much of my sister, Sarah. She was so pretty. Turned heads wherever she went. Her hair was the colour of gold. Pure gold.' Antoinette took a tissue from the box on the coffee table. 'Sorry,' she said, shaking her head and blowing her nose. 'I still get teary-eyed, even now.'

She peered at Grace and frowned. 'Sarah died in a house fire. So young.' The old woman closed her eyes tightly, as if trying to rid her mind of the memories invading it, then continued, 'Of course, no one knows how it works, do they? Maybe when people die they're reborn into the family. Over the years, I've often thought that.' She nodded to herself.

Grace wondered whether Antoinette's sister could be the same "Sarah" who left the note in the jewellery box. A chill ran through her.

'I'm so sorry to hear about your sister dying young. Er... if you don't mind me asking, how old was she?'

'Only eighteen.' Antoinette's eyes swivelled to look at Grace again. 'Seventy years. Time goes so quickly. Doesn't seem that long ago. She was my big sister. I miss her so much.'

Grace closed her eyes briefly. 'I'm sorry,' she said.

'She would have been eighty-eight now. I'm eighty-six. She was going to get married that year. He was called to war. The second world war. Never came back. I think he and Sarah are together now. Happy.' Antoinette smiled, revealing coffee-coloured teeth.

Grace couldn't help smiling back at her; her smile was so genuine and warm.

'Well, that's what I like to believe,' said Antoinette, shrugging. 'As I said before, who really knows?' She leaned forward and pointed at the plate of muffins. 'I made those myself, this morning. My sister used to love cakes. Any kind of cake. Had such a sweet tooth. Please help yourself; and I think the tea must be brewed by now. Would you mind pouring it, dear? My hands are a bit shaky with the arthritis.' She held up a misshapen hand.

Grace picked up the plate of muffins and a small china saucer and held them towards Antoinette.

'Thank you.' With an unsteady hand, Antoinette placed a muffin in the saucer. 'If you could put it there,' she pointed to a small side table next to the sofa. 'It'll be easier for me to reach. Thank you.'

Grace poured some tea for herself and Antoinette, and they

shared a pleasant half-hour together as Antoinette brought her up to date with the neighbourhood gossip.

When Grace returned home, she went straight to the kitchen cupboard and retrieved the jewellery box. Hesitating slightly, she opened the box and took out the piece of paper that now meant so much more and yet remained a mystery. Was *this* written by Antoinette's sister, Sarah? Was Tony the ill fated fiancé who went off to war and never returned?

Grace picked up the little key and twisted it around in her hand.

Sighing, she wondered if she should take the jewellery box next door and ask Antoinette whether she recognised it. That would have to wait, though, because the old woman had said she was expecting her son for dinner.

*

The following morning, Grace was on her way out to visit a friend when Antoinette opened her front door and called out, 'Good morning, Sarah.'

Grace turned around at the sound of the old woman's voice.

'Oh dear, sorry,' said Antoinette, putting a hand over her mouth. 'I wonder why I called you Sarah?' She hung her head and then said, 'I am getting old. Sorry. You know, it must be because I was talking to you about her, yesterday.' She closed the door and walked towards Grace. 'I'm off to the shops. I always get a fresh loaf of bread every day from the bakery. It's a habit. More of a ritual now, I suppose. I don't feel my day has started properly if I don't go out and get a fresh loaf.'

'Wow, a whole loaf of bread in a day. I don't think I get through one a week,' commented Grace, eyes wide.

'My mum used to buy a fresh loaf every day.' Antoinette's

gaze seemed far away for a moment, as if lost back in time. Then, shaking her head, she said, 'Oh, don't worry, it isn't wasted. I feed the birds. Another ritual of mine. I go to the local park every week and feed the ducks. I give some bread to the local children there as well; they love feeding the ducks.' She smiled revealing her coffee-coloured teeth again; in this light they had a marble sheen, and Grace was impressed that although discoloured with age, and slightly chipped in places, they were almost perfectly straight and appeared to be her own. Looking past the wrinkles, she imagined Antoinette must have been quite beautiful as a young woman.

Grace's mind had been working overtime throughout this exchange, trying to find the right time to mention the jewellery box. Without thinking, she said, 'Antoinette, um... I hope you don't mind me asking, but did your sister, Sarah, ever visit my house?'

'Visit?' Antoinette raised her eyebrows. 'We lived there—our family—for about fourteen years. Until the fire. Then our neighbours let us stay with them, here.' She pointed to her own house. 'Our neighbours were relatives of my mother. My mum couldn't bear moving back there after Sarah died, though.'

Grace's eyes widened. 'I... I think I may have found something in the house that belonged to her.'

Antoinette put a hand to her mouth and stared at Grace.

'Um... it's a jewellery box. Silver—'

'With a tortoiseshell design?' said Antoinette, quickly.

'Yes.'

Glancing at her watch, Grace saw that she should have been on the train by now—was meeting up with a friend for lunch. Somehow, though, this struck her as more important; she felt an urge to find out more about the secret of the box.

'Can I see it?' asked Antoinette in a small voice.

Grace noticed tears in the old woman's eyes.

'Of course.'

Grace invited her into her house, and led the way into the kitchen. She took the jewellery box out of the cupboard and sat it on the table.

Antoinette began to cry and fumbled with her sleeve, seemingly searching for a handkerchief.

Grace handed her a tissue from the box on the table.

'Thank you, dear. Sorry.'

'No, please don't apologise. It must be hard to see it again. The memories—'

Antoinette nodded and reached out a shaky hand to open the box. She took out the piece of paper and unfolded it. On doing so, a smile instantly broke through her tears. 'Oh my, I'd completely forgotten about that.' She smiled so brightly her eyes were dancing. 'This... This is wonderful.'

'What is?' Grace shrugged.

The old woman giggled and put a hand to her heart. 'When we were young, Sarah and I made a pact. Can I have this?' she asked, a twinkle in her eye as she held up the piece of paper.

Grace shrugged again, still none the wiser. 'Of course, it's yours after all.'

'I feel so silly, like a little girl again. This has brought back so many memories. You have no idea how great it is to be holding this. Thank you.'

Grace frowned. *It's only a scrap of paper,* she thought to herself. 'Er... what about the key? Do you want it?'

'That's the key to our dolls' house, I think. I've no idea where the dolls' house is.' Antoinette stepped forward and hugged Grace. 'Thank you so much for this. I can hardly believe it.' She closed and opened her eyes in an exaggerated blink.

Antoinette invited Grace to dinner the next evening. Her son was going to be there. Grace got the distinct impression the old woman might be trying to set her up with her son. After all, she had asked if Grace was single. Grace wanted to decline the dinner invitation, but hoped to get more information from Antoinette about the note in the jewellery box, feeling sure there must be a story behind it.

A few minutes after 7 p.m., Grace knocked on her neighbour's door. The door was opened by a teary-eyed man. Antoinette's son. He wiped his eyes on his sleeve and said, 'Hi.

Um, my mum's not well. She hasn't been able to cook. She asked me to apologise to you. She's upstairs in bed.'

'Oh, okay, I'm sorry to hear that.'

'She did want to thank you for returning the letter her sister wrote. Says she'd like a word.' John gestured for Grace to enter.

She followed him through the dimly lit hallway, then up the stairs.

He pointed the way to a room on the right, calling out, 'Mum! Grace is here!'

Somewhat nervously, Grace entered the bedroom. The scent of lavender pervaded the air.

Antoinette was sitting up in bed. As soon as she saw Grace, she beamed and said, 'Hello, dear. Thank you so much for coming.' Her voice sounded hoarse. She coughed. 'I wanted to tell you the story behind the note you found. It means a lot to me, and as you're the one who found it I think it would be nice for you to know. Besides, I really want to tell someone; well, *everyone*. When we were chatting the other day, you said you're a writer.' Antoinette stopped and had a coughing fit. Her eyes began to water.

Grace thought of calling John, worried in case something happened.

'Sorry,' croaked Antoinette. 'Can you pass me that water?' she managed to say in a squeaky voice.

Grace gave her the glass of water that sat on the bedside table.

After Antoinette had drunk some of the water, the redness on her cheeks subsided. 'Oh, I hate those tickly coughs, don't you?' she said, wrinkling her nose.

'Yes,' said Grace, nodding and taking the glass of water from Antoinette's outstretched arm.

'Thank you, dear. Now where was I? Oh, yes; you're a writer?'

'Um... yes, I write novels and short stories; fiction.'

'That's okay. Perhaps you could write up my story as a mystery. Pretend it's fiction. I just think something like this should be told. I'm still finding it hard to believe.'

Grace took a seat beside the bed. 'I have been curious about the note, actually,' she admitted, feeling more able to, knowing the old woman wanted to tell her story.

Grace noticed that Antoinette's eyes had a faraway look, as if her body was present but her thoughts elsewhere.

'Where to begin...?' said the old woman. Then she smiled brightly at Grace before gazing up at the ceiling, a slight crease in her brow.

She turned to face Grace and began to speak: 'Grant Simmons, our late grandfather, was our hero. He died when I was fourteen and Sarah was sixteen. After his funeral, we stayed up all night wondering where Grandpa had gone. We cried so many tears. We couldn't bear the fact we'd never see him again. The chat turned a bit morbid.' Antoinette giggled. 'Sarah and I began to talk about life after death.'

Grace's eyes widened.

'Sarah said something like, "If only Grandpa Grant would send us a sign, you know, say he's still around." Just then—and I can't to this day explain how it happened—the table lamp beside the bed went flying and fell on the floor. Amazingly, it wasn't damaged. Sarah and I took that as a sign from Grandpa Grant.'

'Wow,' said Grace, mouth open.

'Quite.' Antoinette nodded. 'Anyway, a week or so later I asked Sarah if I could have her dolls' house; she hadn't played with it for ages. She said plainly, "You can have the dolls' house when I'm dead, and I'll make sure I give you a sign that I'm still around, like Grandpa did."

'I've been waiting decades for that sign. So, well, now you probably see why the note meant so much to me. Sarah must have left it for me to find. This may sound silly, but for me, finding that note is like proof she has been with me all these years; right here by my side.'

'But she didn't know she would die... I mean, how could she have known she would die before you?' Grace shrugged.

'I'm not sure, dear. Please bear with an old woman with a silly dream,' she said.

'No... I don't think it's silly at all,' said Grace.

'I like to think it's a sign from Sarah.' Antoinette smiled.

Grace frowned. 'So, who was Tony?'

Antoinette laughed. 'That's me. That's what Sarah called me. Started off as a joke and became a nickname.'

'Oh, I see... So, the note—'

'The note was for me. Yes.'

'That's quite a story,' said Grace. 'It certainly makes you think.'

'It does.' Antoinette nodded. 'I've always thought there's something after death. John thinks I'm silly when I talk like this. I knew you'd understand.' She looked into Grace's eyes.

Grace smiled. 'Um... so what happened to the dolls' house?'

'I'm not sure. So much was destroyed in the house fire.'

***

Antoinette's symptoms went from bad to worse over the next few days. John visited her and cooked and cleaned for her. Grace also tried to help out when she could, seeing how weary he was.

A week after Grace had sat in her bedroom chatting with her, Antoinette died in her sleep. John visited Grace to relay the news and tell her the date of the funeral. 'I'm sure she'd want you there,' he said through tears. 'She was so grateful for your help, but more so for giving her the gift of the memory of her late sister. She never stopped talking about it.'

*

After the funeral, Grace and John returned together to Antoinette's house for the wake. Grace had helped him organise everything.

'Thank you so much, Grace,' said John, when they were alone in the house after the guests had left. 'You've been a godsend in all this. You turned up exactly when you were needed. Like an angel. Mum liked you.' He touched her shoulder.

'I'm happy to help,' said Grace, blushing as she glanced shyly at John, realising she was developing feelings for him.

She averted her eyes from his.

'I really appreciate your help,' he said in an almost-whisper.

Grace looked up at him again and was lost in his dark brown eyes.

They stared into each other's eyes for what seemed like minutes to Grace, but must have been only a few seconds.

John leaned towards her and kissed her firmly on the lips. She could not help but return his kiss. For a few moments they were locked into each other, eyes closed, in a passionate embrace.

Slowly, John pulled away, eyes wide. 'I'm so sorry. I don't know what happened.'

'It's okay,' soothed Grace, touching his cheek softly.

'Are you feeling sorry for me because of what happened...? Mum—'

'No. I think we've been... Well, we're getting on well.'

'We are.'

Grace smiled.

'I'd like us to keep in touch,' he said.

'I'd like that too.'

*

Over the next few weeks, John made the decision to move into his late mother's house. Grace helped with some of the unpacking, and met his children. She began to feel as if they could have a future together. Everything in her life was slipping into place. Memories of Antoinette often entered her mind; she felt happy to have known her, even for that brief period of time.

Whilst thinking about such things one evening, walking into her house, she accidentally grazed her knee on a box in the hallway. It was a box of bric-a-brac. She'd intended to store it away until she could decide what to do with it, but the staircase was full and her ladder wasn't tall enough to access the loft.

Rubbing her knee to avoid the inevitable bruise, Grace dialled John's number. 'Hi, oh nothing much,' she answered when he picked up the phone and asked her what she was up to.

'Listen, you have a ladder, don't you? Would you come over

and help me put some of my stuff in the loft, please? It's blocking my hallway and I've just bashed my knee into one of the boxes.'

Later that evening, John arrived, and they took turns climbing up the ladder into the loft to organise Grace's bric-a-brac.

It was very dark in the loft, so they used a torch. The light shining from the torch was dim. Grace couldn't wait to get it over with. She piled her belongings as near to the hatch as possible for easy access should she wish to get them down at any time.

The area near the hatch was getting too full and it became obvious that access to the loft would be hindered if everything was piled close to the edge. She walked further into the loft, shining the light into her path.

As the light reached the back of the attic, Grace saw a table lamp. Then, suddenly and inexplicably, the lamp fell as if thrown and landed on the loft floor in front of her with a loud crash. Startled, she took a couple of steps back. Her mind went back to her conversation with Antoinette. Could this be a sign from the old woman? Grace shivered.

'What was that?' shouted John from his position next to the ladder.

'Er... nothing!'

As her heart's pace gradually returned to normal, Grace took a deep breath and leaned over to pick up the table lamp. Did she step on its cable, perhaps, and cause it to topple over? No, that wasn't it. Perhaps there had been a gust of wind; maybe the roof had a loose tile letting the wind through. The lamp didn't appear to have been damaged; even the glass bulb remained intact as far as she could see. Grace shrugged and walked towards the back of the loft. A large rectangular object came into view. Shining her torch, she saw clearly: a dolls' house.

Grace's mouth fell open. *This must be Sarah's dolls' house.* She placed a hand over her mouth and her heart began to flutter.

'John!' she shouted. 'Come up here! I need you to help me with something!'

'What's happened? Are you okay?' He climbed through into the loft.

'I'm fine,' she said. 'Look! It's your mum's dolls' house. Well, it belonged to her sister.'

'Oh, wow!' His eyes widened. 'She thought it was destroyed in the fire.'

'I know. Let's take it downstairs. I know where the key is.'

Together, they managed to carry the large dolls' house down the ladder in one piece.

Out of breath when they arrived the bottom, Grace said, 'Do you know where your mum put the jewellery box?'

'What jewellery box?' he shrugged and regarded her blankly.

'An old jewellery box I found in the house when I moved in. I gave it to your mum when I visited... The last time I saw her. Thought she should have it.'

John shook his head.

Grace spoke quickly, 'It's a pretty little box, with a tortoiseshell design. Silver. The key to the dolls' house is inside it.'

'I think I saw something like that in her bedroom—'

'Great! Can you go and get it, please?'

Grace sat waiting for John to return, biting her fingernails and staring at the dolls' house. The wooden structure had once been painted pink or purple, but the dust that covered it now made the colour hard to determine. Grace sneezed a few times and was blowing her nose when John returned to the room holding the jewellery box.

Grace leapt towards him and took the box. Opening it, she snatched the tiny key and held it in front of her.

'That's the key to the dolls' house?' he asked, frowning.

'Yes,' she replied, her eyebrows raised. 'Just think, this little house hasn't been opened for about seventy years! This is so exciting, isn't it?'

'If you say so,' he said, chuckling.

Grace's hand shook slightly as she inserted the key into the lock. Adrenaline raced through her. She pulled open the door with a wide smile.

At the front of the dolls' house there were two miniature dolls, but what Grace noticed first was the note on a scrap of paper, like the one that had been in the jewellery box, written by the same hand: Sarah's. It read, simply, *"Tony and Sarah, together, for ever."*

Tragedy of Love

The freedom and exhilaration of that final step merged with fear and regret beckoning her to change her mind, but it was too late. The train screeched to a halt, but too late. Too late.

Alone, unloved; that's how she felt. That's why she did it. No one would understand. That's why she didn't tell anyone. It had been coming for weeks, for months. Maybe years.

Older. Time moving on, others moving on. Her life static. Invisible. That's how she felt. Time kept moving on. Wouldn't wait. Wouldn't give her a chance to catch up... to be like the rest... to be "normal". But did she want to be like the rest? No. Maybe that was why she did it. No one would ever know. No one could ask her now. It was too late.

A question remained in the background. Made her uncomfortable in the presence of other people. Was there something wrong with her? There must be. Was that why no one cared? No one wanted her.

Most of the time, she was happy. Then someone would question her, ask why she was alone. It's about time. Should be looking for someone; should be married. Should have children. Maybe wear some make-up, lose weight, go out more. Not offering to go out with her, of course. Advice of the uncaring.

Endless days, endless nights. Alone.

Shouldn't have said that, shouldn't have done that, should do this, should do that. Maybe that's why she went against the grain. Ended it all.

***

Philip stepped out into the gloomy October morning and grumbled as he struggled to get his umbrella out of his bag. Always raining. Today was the day; he would ask her to go out to dinner with him. They'd worked together for two years now. Two years, come December. There'd been flirting, or had there? He wasn't sure; daren't make a move. Only in the last two weeks had he felt a compulsion to say something *before it's too late*. Possibly because that young lad had started work in the IT department and he'd seen him talking to her.

Philip had liked her from the first day they met. They were introduced by Mr Spence, the manager.

They worked in offices on opposite sides of the building, but often crossed in the hallway. A shy hello at first, then a few words about the weather, a bit of gossip: 'Did you hear so-and-so is leaving?', 'Did you see what so-and-so did yesterday in the staff canteen?'

He'd nearly asked her to dance with him, the year before, at the office Christmas party. She'd been dancing with a couple of colleagues. She looked so comfortable out there, smiling, having fun. He lost his nerve at the last minute. He'd never been very good at dancing and didn't want to make a fool of himself.

But today he would ask her out.

As he arrived at the Tube station platform, he heard an announcement, 'There are severe delays on the Northern Line due to a person under a train.'

He checked the time on his watch. *Going to be late again.*

*

He didn't see her that day, or the next. Perhaps she was on holiday.

He never saw her again. Weeks went by. Had she left? Unusual: if someone was leaving, there'd be an e-mail announcing it, collections for a gift, a card to sign. There was nothing.

A couple of months later, he enquired about her.

'Oh, she left, I think,' said Sophie, the receptionist. 'She was a nice girl, but a bit too quiet. Don't think she even told us she was leaving.'

'Who's that?' asked Mark, one of the security guards.

'You remember, Selene, the girl who used to work in Clara's department,' said Sophie.

'Oh, yeah. The blonde. No, she died.'

Sophie's eyes popped wide open and she placed a hand in front of her mouth.

Philip twisted around to face Mark. 'Died?' he repeated the word, unbelieving, shaking his head.

'Yeah,' said Mark, nodding. 'Her dad phoned Clara when it happened. She wanted to keep it quiet; to respect the family's wishes. I saw her when she was heading out to the funeral. She said the girl threw herself under a train.' He shrugged. 'It's the quiet ones you have to look out for, hey?'

Philip felt tears in his eyes. 'Well, I'd b-better get back to work,' he said, his voice breaking slightly.

Sophie, a hand still in front of her mouth, nodded at him.

The Beach

When the mist cleared there was no sign of Toyah.

Mike shook the salt water from his hair and rubbed his eyes. He shivered. There was an ice-cold chill to the air. It was cold and dark. Mere moments before, they had been laughing and joking as they splashed water at each other. They drifted out from the beach, but were both good swimmers, no need to fear the depth of the sea. Or so he had thought. *Where is she?*

There was nothing but sea for miles around. Grey and black in parts. The sky, a deep blue-grey, threatened a storm. *Where am I?* thought Mike, puzzled. Panic threatened to engulf him, but he knew he needed to stay calm, had to find Toyah.

Someone rose out of the water; a woman. *Toyah?* No, it wasn't. This woman's hair was darker, or could that be because it had been soaked in the water? 'Toyah?' he asked.

The woman turned towards him, her eyes deep and black, her skin and lips a sickly shade of blue. She disappeared back into the sea.

What's going on?

The water became icier by the minute, chilling him to the bone. *I won't get out of this alive.* 'I will, I will, I will get out!' he said out loud to drown out the negative thoughts. 'Toyah! Toyah! Can you hear me?'

'Of course I can, silly. What's wrong with you?'

He opened his eyes and saw Toyah standing there, by the door leading into the en-suite in their hotel bedroom.

He sat up in bed and his eyes swept the room.

'Were you having a bad dream or something?'

It was only a dream. He forced a smile at Toyah. 'Must have been,' he replied. Something nagged him, something he could not quite get a grasp of, way back in the recesses of his mind.

'So, are you planning on getting out of bed today?' she asked, giggling.

*

Mike sat across from Toyah at the kitchen table and sipped his coffee. The noise of the traffic on the street below was a far cry from the peace and tranquility of their hotel room in Spain, but somehow he felt a great relief to be back here in London, no longer having to worry about what his dream had meant.

The nearest sea was miles away, and the weather here hardly ever warm enough to bother visiting the beach, let alone attempting to swim in the sea. While these factors were reassuring, it was unsettling that his dream had frightened and haunted him so.

He'd had precognitive dreams when he was younger. It worried him that this one still lingered somewhere in his mind no matter how hard he tried to forget it, as if it were some kind of message he was unable to decipher.

'It's a bit early for you to be working, isn't it?' he grumbled, as Toyah typed on the keyboard of her laptop.

She glanced up at him, and rolled her eyes. 'I'm a writer, what do you expect? I have to write when the inspiration grabs me.'

'Are you being inspired by me drinking my coffee?'

'Be quiet, or I'll write a scene where you spill the coffee on your hand, scalding yourself.'

'Sometimes I think you love your laptop more than me,' he said, tutting.

Toyah narrowed her eyes at him as if in thought. 'I don't,' she began. Then she sighed. 'But I love writing more.'

He hung his head.

'Sorry, I didn't mean that,' she added quickly. 'Anyway, I'm not writing my novel at the moment, I'm going to write a review about the hotel we stayed in.'

'A review of the hotel? Why?'

'Well, I thought it was nice; the staff were friendly. There's this travel site where you can review places you've stayed.'

'You're weird.'

Toyah giggled. 'Yeah, well, writers are supposed to be weird, aren't they? Anyway, what's wrong with writing a review about the hotel? Reviews are important.'

'No they're not.'

Toyah screwed up her face. 'When you're going to buy something, don't you look at the reviews first?'

'Not really.'

'I'm sure you do. You at least read a write-up about what you're going to buy, don't you?'

Mike shrugged.

'I never realised how important reviews were until I started publishing my books. The more reviews you have, the more people take notice of the product. It's the same for small businesses, like this hotel we stayed at. They need reviews.'

'Whatever,' said Mike, standing up. 'I'm going to start getting ready for work.'

'No, no, wait. I need your input.' Toyah peered at the kitchen clock. 'You've still got a few minutes, haven't you?'

Mike sighed and sat down. 'Okay, five minutes, then I've gotta go.'

'Okay.' Toyah squinted at the PC. 'Right, I've found the site. Our hotel was "Sunnyside Beach Hotel". Here, look, there are some reviews already. Two five star ones. I'm going to give it five stars. Hang on... what's this? One star? What was wrong?' Toyah began to read the review in a condescending tone:

'*"I stayed in this excuse for a hotel and they didn't tell me about the danger at the local beach. I could have died! Lucky for me I wasn't interested in swimming..."* What's he going on about?' questioned Toyah.

Mike knitted his brows. 'Carry on. Read the rest.'

'Sounds like a moaning idiot to me,' said Toyah. 'Oh, okay, let's see what else he says: *"The only way I found out about the danger was from overhearing two of the long-term residents at the hotel talking about the sea. That resort is known for having whirlpools. A girl who stayed in room fifteen last year, drowned..."* '

Toyah's mouth fell open. 'Um... fifteen was our room...'

Mike stared at her, eyes wide. His face blanched. The eyes of the woman in his dream stared back at him through Toyah's gaze.

Betrayal

Desiree pulled her coat tighter around her in a vain attempt to battle against the wind, and the chill she felt inside. Today's visit was impromptu, but one that had been a long time coming. It was time to try to build a bridge, if not for her own peace of mind, for the sake of tying up loose ends, making sure no one would suffer unnecessarily.

She stopped at the gate to number 8, Wandsworth Drive, and stared at the house. In the past, she had never felt welcome here. What would his reaction be?

Taking a deep breath, knowing it would not calm her racing heart, she shuffled towards the door. There was nothing to lose now.

With a trembling hand, she rang the bell, then quickly put both hands in her pockets to hide any sign of nerves.

The net curtain in the window to her left fluttered slightly. Tension built up as she waited to find out if the door would be opened, or would they choose to ignore her?

'Go away,' came the female voice through the letterbox. 'You're not welcome here.'

Desiree stiffened. She opened her mouth to reply, but then thought better of it and turned to leave. Tears threatened to fall, burning the edges of her eyes. The wind was still blustery and she noticed it all the more as she stepped off the doorstep towards the gate.

At least she could say she'd tried. But had she? Wasn't it cowardly to walk away? Something made her stop walking.

Three years. Three whole years. Surely even Rolanda couldn't hold a grudge that long.

Desiree forced herself to approach the house again. With an even shakier hand she pressed the doorbell one more time. This time, the door swung open on its hinges almost immediately.

Rolanda stood before her, hands on hips, red-faced. 'What is it you don't understand about "go away"? Did I not make it clear enough? You are not welcome here!' She said the last five words in a snake-like hiss, her eyes narrowed, piercing through Desiree's stare.

If looks could kill, thought Desiree, morosely.

After her outburst, Rolanda stood surveying Desiree with a sullen frown.

Not unusual for her, thought Desiree, trying to remember the last time she'd seen Rolanda smile. She could not recall.

'P-please, Rolanda. I came here to see you and Dad, and ask if you'd forgive me, just this one last time.'

Rolanda averted her eyes, pursed her lips, and sneered, 'Why should we?'

Desiree hung her head. In truth, she didn't feel she was the one to blame, and had only phrased her sentence "forgive me" knowing how stubborn Rolanda could be. She closed her eyes briefly, then looked up at Rolanda again. The woman didn't meet her eyes, but instead glanced at her watch, and ran her fingers through her unruly, coarse, blonde hair.

'I wanted to say I'm sorry for any offence I might have caused,' said Desiree. 'Want to let you know I'm not upset, not angry anymore.'

'Huh!' Rolanda rolled her eyes, took a step backwards, and grasped the front door handle. 'I don't know why you were so angry in the first place. I think you're crazy and I don't want you anywhere near my home, my husband, or my children. You're obviously in need of psychiatric help.' With that, she slammed the door.

Desiree stood in stunned silence, eyes glued to the closed

door. She wanted to shake Rolanda, wanted to scream. Rolanda always managed to rile her, to awaken a real frustration within her, in the way she came out with so many statements holding herself out to be superior.

Desiree had been over it and over it in her mind since the day, three years ago, when matters came to a head. Each time they'd met, Rolanda had added one more drop of poison, building up to a toxic meltdown. Desiree shook her head. *If anyone needs psychiatric help, it's her. There's no getting through to her.*

She didn't know much about Rolanda's background, except that her parents were wealthy, and she had a snooty air about her; also, there seemed to be an inbuilt insecurity that kept her on the defensive most of the time.

Eight years before, Rolanda walked into Desiree's father's life, quite soon after his divorce from Desiree's mother.

Craig, her father, had been a teenager—fifteen years old—when Desiree was born. Her grandparents forced the young couple to marry, embarrassed to have an illegitimate child in the family. How times had changed.

The marriage was doomed from the start. Desiree's parents were constantly fighting. Her mother resented getting pregnant at such a young age and would moan about it all the time. Desiree's father would retaliate with: 'Why didn't you have an abortion then?'

Desiree would listen uncomfortably to these spats from her bedroom, tears in her eyes.

They never had any more children. As far as Desiree knew, they slept in separate beds. They divorced when Desiree was twenty years old. She knew her father had many affairs, and suspected her mother must have too. She often thought it odd that her parents had stayed together for so long.

When Rolanda turned up, shortly after the divorce, Desiree had a sneaking suspicion that the woman may have been the reason for her parents finally splitting up.

Rolanda had no interest in Desiree at all, but made a show of caring about her for a while. As soon as the engagement ring was on her finger she changed completely, ignoring Desiree, treating her as if she were a pest, in the way.

Desiree aired a grievance about the way Rolanda treated her, to her father, a couple of times, getting quite emotional in the process. This didn't go down well with Rolanda who began to complain that Desiree was a troublemaker.

Rolanda was only a few years older than her, and this exacerbated the problem; Desiree often thought Rolanda behaved immaturely. When she mentioned that to her father in a heated argument, Rolanda threatened to leave him, and he subsequently warned Desiree to behave or to stay away from the wedding.

It felt like betrayal to Desiree—her own father not wanting her at his wedding, and sticking up for his fiancée over her. Rolanda had been causing the problems all along, but whenever Desiree tried to tell her father this, he would say she was "imagining" it.

Desiree reluctantly attended the wedding and was left feeling like an outsider. She hadn't been asked to participate in the ceremony in any way, even though Rolanda's daughter was a bridesmaid.

'She's only a little girl. Little girls like being bridesmaids,' said her father, when Desiree confronted him about it.

'What if I wanted to be a bridesmaid too?' she retorted, tears in her eyes.

He closed his eyes briefly, then glared at her. 'Where has all this jealousy come from, Desi?' he asked. 'You really need to pull yourself together and act your age. I won't let you come between me and Rolanda. She's my wife and you have to accept that.'

Desiree stood open-mouthed for a moment and watched him walk away, back to his bride who was busy shaking hands with the wedding guests. *She's so fake*, thought Desiree. She couldn't understand how this rake-thin woman with premature wrinkles and the ugliest coarse hair she'd ever seen, could have ensnared her father and kept such a grip on him. *It can't be her personality he's in love with*, she mused. As she was thinking that, her eyes settled on Erina, who was playing catch with one of the other bridesmaids using a decorative balloon.

It struck her—not for the first time—how much Erina

resembled her father. The same curly black hair. Was this little girl the reason he devoted himself to the cold and irritating Rolanda?

Desiree ordered a birth certificate and found out Erina was indeed her half-sister. When she confronted her father about it, he denied any knowledge.

Rolanda said she was a "nosey, good-for-nothing meddler" and accused her of trying to destroy her marriage.

Desiree was banned from visiting the house not long afterwards.

Rolanda soon became pregnant again.

When the baby, a girl, was born, Desiree visited the house taking a gift. She was met with an icy reception, and over the next few months became increasingly frustrated at not being allowed to be more involved in her sisters' lives. Whenever she phoned to arrange a visit she was invariably told they were busy.

Her frustration turned to anger and culminated in a heated argument at her father's house when Desiree turned up with a birthday present for Erina on her sixth birthday and found a house full of guests enjoying a birthday party to which she hadn't been invited.

She ended up causing a scene, and throwing a bowl of punch over Rolanda in front of a few children.

The ban on her visiting the house was then enforced for the "foreseeable future".

Desiree never thought of visiting them after that. Until today, three years later. Now she wished she hadn't bothered.

Tears streamed down Desiree's cheeks as she walked away from the house. Some passersby on the crowded streets appeared to want to comfort her, but none of them did. Others averted their gaze as soon as their eyes met hers. Not one person stopped to ask if she needed help. This was London, after all. No one speaks to strangers.

Would it have made a difference if she'd told Rolanda the real reason for her visit? She felt a tug at her heart wondering if there would have been a different outcome had her father answered the door instead of Rolanda. Shaking her head, she erased those thoughts. The time for emotions had passed. He had chosen sides; she was no longer important to him.

As Desiree walked past a shop on the way to the Tube station, a beautiful red coat in the window display caught her eye. It looked so luxurious. Her own coat was threadbare and hardly kept the wind out. The shop was a designer fashion store, the price tag would be expensive, but she couldn't remember the last time she'd bought something on impulse. A yearning burned inside her.

She walked into the store, and although feeling faint, tried on the coat and managed to somehow survive the long queue of customers. Every single experience in her life now had become something to cherish. Even the simple act of standing in a queue with other people. How long would she have left to do this?

After Desiree bought the coat, she changed out of her old one, putting it into the carrier bag she'd been given by the shop assistant.

Passing a charity shop, Desiree made the decision to leave her old coat in there.

The new red coat felt wonderfully warm against her skin. She hardly noticed the wind and couldn't help smiling to herself. Even with her weakness taking more and more of a hold on her, she made it to the Tube station, onto the train, and all the way to her destination.

Exiting the Tube station, she once again felt the benefit of her lovely new coat.

It was starting to get dark.

As she turned the corner into her street, she nearly bumped into a young boy. 'Sorry,' she mumbled.

Just then, he flicked open the blade on his knife and pointed it at her. 'Give me your money,' he said.

Her eyes widened as paranoia took hold. *How does he know I've got money?* Then, looking him up and down, she guessed he was an opportunist, seeing her expensive coat and assuming she must be rich.

'I ain't joking, lady, give me your money, or I'll stab you.'

'I'm dying,' she heard herself say, 'Now, or in two months, won't make a difference; in fact you'll probably be doing me a favour. You see, every day I get weaker and weaker. One day soon, I won't be able to stand up; I'll be in hospital, until they switch off the life support, probably.' She gazed upwards, noticing for the first time in a long time, how lovely the sky appeared at sunset.

'You're crazy,' said the boy.

'Knowing you're going to die soon can do that to a person,' she said.

The boy walked away muttering something to himself.

Desiree almost wanted to call him back, beg him to follow through with his threat. How much more eloquent and satisfying it would have been to die here, in a pool of blood to match her new red coat, instead of on some cold hospital bed in a sterilised ward, totally oblivious on medication.

*

She kept her appointment with the solicitor the next day, knowing she had to do this now; couldn't put it off anymore. Denial was one thing, but having people who didn't care about her laughing and dancing on her grave was entirely another.

'I want to leave everything to my mum,' she said to the solicitor.

'Everything?' the solicitor said, raising an eyebrow, 'But Ms Juno—'

'It's *my* will,' snapped Desiree, and then immediately regretted the outburst. 'Sorry.'

'I understand this is a difficult matter to discuss,' started the solicitor, 'but, well, the likelihood is, your mother will die before you.'

She won't die before me, thought Desiree, but didn't say anything. *Unless she walks in front of a bus, or kills herself when she hears the news...*

'We need to cover every eventuality. If your mother were to die before you, who would—'

'I'll be dead within a few months; that's the prognosis,' said Desiree, staring blankly ahead. 'There's nothing that can be done. Soon, I'll probably be too ill to look after myself.'

The solicitor, a young woman with the slightest hint of grey at her temple, and normally quite rosy-cheeked, paled. Tears began to form in her brown eyes, her mouth agape. She regained her immaculate composure in less than a minute. If Desiree had not been staring at her, she would have missed any signs of disconcertedness. The solicitor was a professional, barely human.

Desiree almost felt sorry for the woman, feeling sure that all this restriction of emotion must be bad for her health.

'Right. So, you want to leave everything to your mother? I'll get my secretary to type it up, and you can sign it before you leave,' said the solicitor, quickly, as if she feared Desiree would collapse and die right here and now in her office.

Desiree held the will in her hand. She hadn't even reached the age of thirty. Would never know what it was like to be a thirty-something, or have a fortieth birthday party. Morbid thoughts followed her along the street as she walked away from the solicitor's office.

She wondered what her mother would spend the money on. She'd always been thrifty; would probably leave it in the bank to rot. *Better than those two getting their hands on it*, thought Desiree bitterly, as images of her father and Rolanda entered her mind.

Over three million. The amount sitting in her bank account right now. Over three million pounds won on the lottery the month before. She hadn't told anyone, because the win came just a couple of days after she learned the devastating news about her health. Most days getting out of bed was a task, but she'd forced herself to carry on going to work, trying to deny there was anything wrong with her. She'd succeeded, until almost fainting in the office two days before and making up a lie, saying she thought it was flu. Her boss had agreed to her taking a couple of days off to recover. It finally hit her then that it was time to face facts.

She pulled her coat closer, against the wind, knowing the chill she felt came mostly from inside. Her head ached. Feeling nauseated, she sat at a bus stop to catch her breath.

Putting a hand on her forehead, she lost her grip on the will. It took flight on the wind. She was not strong enough to run after it. *I'll have to go back to the solicitor. Get another copy,* she thought, wearily.

Panic took hold: no one knew about the will. If she died now, right here, no one would ever know. Rolanda would spend that money. *She's got expensive taste, buying the latest fashions.*

Desiree turned back towards the high street, wanting to return to the solicitor's office, but her mind went blank. She couldn't remember where it was. *Isn't that strange?* she thought, *I've only just left... Where is it?*

She turned around 360 degrees, bemused, her mind muddled. The turning around made her dizzy. Everything went hazy.

Desiree awoke in hospital. Next to the bed sat her father. When she opened her eyes, he leaned forward.

'Desi, are you okay?'

'Why—' Desiree tried to speak, but found her voice was hoarse. Coughing, she tried again, 'Why are you here?' She pursed her lips.

'The hospital called me. You had me in your contacts on your phone.'

'Where's Mum?'

'She's on her way.'

Desiree turned her face away.

'Why didn't you tell us you were ill?' he said.

She glared at him. 'Er... and when exactly was I supposed to have told you? You banned me from your house, remember?'

'Yes... Yes, well... That was a mistake. Rolanda and I—'

'What's that bitch got to do with it?'

Just then, Rolanda appeared from behind the curtain that had been partially closed around Desiree's bed.

'I'm sorry for everything, Desi. I really am. I'll make up for it, you'll see.' Rolanda, smiling brightly, walked over to Desiree and took her hand. 'I treated you unfairly from the start. It was my fault. Your dad loves you. Look, you're a part of our family and when you're better I want you to come and live with us.'

Desiree felt sure she must be dreaming or hallucinating, and began to think she must have been given some strong drugs. She stared blankly at Rolanda.

'Yes, we'd like that, if you want to,' said her father.

'Why the sudden change?' huffed Desiree. Her brow furrowed as she looked at the two of them.

Her father glanced at Rolanda and then said, quickly, 'It's not sudden; Rolanda and I were feeling bad for—'

'Yes, we were,' said Rolanda, squeezing Desiree's hand. 'We felt so bad for leaving you out.'

'Well, I don't need to live with you, but I do want to be able to visit my sisters—'

'Of course, of course, anything you want,' said Rolanda.

A nurse arrived, interrupting them, announcing that the doctor wanted to see Desiree and they would have to wait in the visitors' area.

'What have you told my dad?' Desiree asked the nurse when her two unwelcome visitors were out of earshot.

'We told him you fainted.'

'Does he know about... you know... my illness?'

'No. We haven't told him, as far as I know.' The nurse closed her eyes briefly, then regarded Desiree with a caring frown. 'Sometimes it's best to tell those we love. You can't leave it too late. They deserve time to get used to this news. It will be worse if they don't know... you know, when the end comes.'

Desiree nodded. She knew the nurse meant well, but it didn't add up that the woman who had so rudely rejected her a couple of days before was being so nice to her now if she merely thought she'd fainted.

'We've given your handbag and coat to your dad. He's looking after them, so don't worry,' said the nurse.

'Okay, thank you,' said Desiree, distractedly.

After she had been seen by the doctor, Desiree was taken back to the ward and found her mother had joined the visitors beside her bed.

'Hello, darling, how are you feeling?' she asked.

'Fine,' said Desiree, the nurse's words ringing in her ears. She felt bad for not telling her mother about the prognosis.

'The nurse says you can go home,' said her mother brightly, but her sullen demeanour betrayed her concern.

'Great,' said Desiree, trying to sound as happy as she could.

They left the hospital arm in arm, being followed awkwardly along the corridor by her father and Rolanda.

At the hospital exit, her father said, 'We'd like to invite you to dinner this Sunday, Desi.'

Desiree turned to face him.

'We need to make amends,' said Rolanda smiling that smile again.

It was strange to see her smile. Rolanda's face appeared odd, as if the smile was out of place.

Desiree's mother took the handbag and coat from her father. 'Thank you for looking after these.'

'A pleasure,' he said.

Desiree and her mother walked away towards the car. Desiree could not help peering over her shoulder in wonder at the two people who were suddenly wanting to be part of her life again.

When Desiree sat in the passenger seat, her mother started the car and asked, before saying another word, 'Why didn't you tell me?'

Desiree's mouth fell open. How did she find out? The nurse had assured her they hadn't told anyone.

'Keeping something like that from your own mother. I can't believe you, Desi.'

'Sorry, Mum.'

'So when were you going to tell me? You've known for a

month now, haven't you?'

'Well...'

'Well?'

'It's not something you can just come out and say.'

'I would be shouting it from the rooftops! Three million pounds. Wow!'

Desiree's eyes widened. 'H-how did you find out?'

'In the most embarrassing way possible. Your dad accused me of keeping it from him and wanting the money for myself.'

'Dad? What's he got to do with it?'

'He's the one who looked in your handbag. Found your bank statement. To be fair, I think he wanted to help the doctors because they asked if you were taking any medication and he didn't know, so he checked the bag to see if there was anything in there. Well, that's what he said, anyway. For all I know, it might have been Rolanda's idea to look in the bag. Nosey cow. But really! Have I taught you nothing? Why were you carrying that in your handbag?'

'I. I needed it. I went to see a solicitor.' It all began to make sense now; the reason they wanted to know her. The money. That's all it was. Her heart sank.

'What did you need to see a solicitor for?'

Desiree glanced briefly at her mother and then turned back to gaze out of the passenger window. 'It's none of your business.'

'Just like telling me you'd won millions was none of my business. I can't understand why you'd keep something like that to yourself. It's not as if I'm going to take it from you, is it?'

'I wasn't ready to tell anyone. Didn't want anything to change.'

'Well, everything changes when you win three million. So, have you decided what you're going to do with it? You have to be sensible. It might seem like an endless supply of money, but these days it's not that much.'

'It's three million, Mum!'

'Yes, but if you go around buying lots of expensive stuff, you'll use it up in no time.'

They drove in silence for a few minutes and then her

mother said. 'You should buy a nice house, in the country. A holiday home, too. You could start up your own business. I've always dreamt of owning a bookshop, with a coffee shop inside, and maybe a gift shop. We could run it together, what do you say?'

'Mum.'

'Sorry, it's your money.'

'Don't worry, you'll get your share,' she said.

'You know, Desi, I think the first thing we... *you* should do, is book a holiday. You're looking pasty.'

'I've just come out of hospital.'

'I've noticed it for a few weeks now, though. You look... I don't know... ill. Are you on one of those fad diets?'

'No!' snapped Desiree.

'Okay, don't bite my head off. Maybe you're overworked. A holiday would do you good.'

'Maybe,' said Desiree, continuing to stare out of the window at the world that would soon be a place she once lived. She used to hate the busy streets, the people who were all in such a hurry to get to where they were going that they often forgot their manners. The cold mornings, the endless rain, the dark evenings. The repetitive station announcements, the delays on her commute to and from work, the never-ending roadworks. The queues in supermarkets. The screaming babies and loud children in crowded streets and shops. But now, she wanted to collect all of those things, hold them close to her. Keep them sacred, not let them go. The fuse had been lit and slowly burned away; like a timed device set to explode at some time in the near future. It was a countdown, the exact end date as yet unknown. She was constantly aware of the presence of the thing that would take her away from all she had ever known. It made her want to hold on tighter.

'Are you going to your dad's on Sunday?' Her mother's voice broke through her reverie.

Desiree took a moment to consider the question. Should she? Then she remembered she might not see any of them again. She wouldn't be concerned if she never saw her father and

Rolanda, but the girls—her sisters—she wanted to see. One last time.

'I will, but only to see Erina and the baby. Don't even know what her name is,' said Desiree, bluntly.

'Jessica,' said her mother.

'They're only interested in my money.'

'Yes... well... I won't comment.'

The next day, Desiree went back to the solicitor's office; this time she asked her mother to drive her, to avoid making the journey alone. She felt tired, and didn't want to end up in hospital again.

'I don't have an appointment,' Desiree told the receptionist, 'but was wondering if I could get a copy of my will. I came here yesterday, but somehow mislaid my copy on the way home.'

'Of course, I'll get that done for you, Ms Juno, please take a seat.'

Back in the car, Desiree's mother peered at her. 'You still haven't told me why you had to go to the solicitor.'

'I don't have to tell you everything, do I?' she replied, holding her handbag closer to her. It contained the will that left all her worldly goods to her mother.

Sunday at her father's house was a chance to see her sisters; something denied her for far too long. She resented the lost years, aware that she would never have a chance to get to know them; no longer because of bitter disputes, but because of the illness eating away at her from the inside. Who knew how much time remained? A month? Two months? A bit longer if she was lucky?

'How are you feeling?' was the first thing Rolanda said to her, putting an arm around her, when she walked into the house. 'Let me get your coat. Do you want a nice cup of tea? It's cold out there, isn't it?'

Fussing, that's what it was, thought Desiree. And only because they wanted to get their hands on her money.

Thinking about it from that angle, they were pathetic. She wished she could be around after her death to see their faces when they found out all the money had been bequeathed to her mother. She had left instructions with the will, stating that she wanted Erina and Jessica to benefit in some way, when they were older; for some money to be put towards their education and welfare.

After the smalltalk was done, they all sat down for dinner.

'I'm going to go shopping with the girls for new clothes soon, Desi; do you want to come?' asked Rolanda.

'Um... it depends, I'm working and—'

'We can go on a weekend; a Saturday would be good.' Rolanda sighed, 'Clothes are so expensive these days, though; we'll have to buy the bare minimum. I feel so bad for the little angels.' She smiled at the children.

Desiree knew she was expecting her to offer to pay. 'I'm sure you'll find something. Primark is cheap and they have some nice stuff,' she said.

Rolanda nearly choked on the champagne they had obviously bought as a sweetener. She gaped at Desiree wide-eyed.

Her father, seeing Rolanda's countenance and most likely fearing an argument would begin, interjected: 'Would anyone like more potatoes?'

'No, I'm full,' said Desiree.

'But we've just started eating,' he said.

'I'm still not feeling well, perhaps I shouldn't have come,' she replied, reaching into her lap to remove the napkin she'd placed there. Dropping the napkin onto the table, she made to stand up.

'Wait,' said Rolanda. 'We have so much catching up to do.' She shot a look at Desiree's father.

He coughed. 'Yes, yes. We want to hear all about what you've been up to these past few years. We shouldn't have lost touch.'

'Whose fault was that?' said Desiree, in a mumble.

Rolanda narrowed her eyes, but stated, 'We want you to be

a part of the girls' lives, Desi. You're their big sister. You should spend more time with them.'

'I agree,' said her father. 'In fact, why don't you take them shopping for clothes next week? It'll give you the chance to get to know them. On your own.'

'Great idea!' Rolanda raised her champagne glass. 'I'll drink to that.'

'You'd like that, wouldn't you girls?' said her father.

The children, who had been busy chatting between themselves as they ate their food, turned towards Desiree and smiled. A tear came to her eye. In a completely different set of circumstances, she would have taken them shopping and bought them whatever they wanted, despite the fact the money-grabbing adults would like nothing better. She would do it for her sisters. But she was dying, and didn't want to form a bond that could not be sustained. It wasn't fair on them. She'd promised herself this would be the one and only visit. A kind of good-bye.

Desiree coughed to clear her throat and said, 'Before we continue with the conversation, I think there's something you should know.'

'Go on,' said her father.

'When I won the lottery, it came as a big shock to me.'

'You won the lottery?' he asked.

Desiree rolled her eyes and sighed. 'Mum told me you already know, so—'

'Oh, um...'

'You saw my bank statement.'

'Yes.' He lowered his head.

'So you knew I had a lot of money.'

'I had no idea,' said Rolanda.

'Yes, well,' continued Desiree, looking from Rolanda to her father. 'I couldn't handle being that rich. I was afraid people would only want to know me because I had money. I panicked, I suppose.'

She ran her fingers along the design on the rose-patterned tablecloth. 'I gave the money away.' She shrugged.

'What?' Her father's eyes popped wide open.

Rolanda gasped. 'All of it?'

Desiree's gaze rested on her hands. 'No, of course not all of it. I gave some to Mum. The rest I gave to charity. It's gone to the best place really, if you think about it.'

'Charity?' Her father wrinkled his nose. 'You're pulling our legs, aren't you?'

'No. I have a friend whose mother is dying. She's sick. Has some unpronounceable disease. Anyway, the hospice where she's being cared for needed a new roof, and they also have a fund for the hospital that researches into the disease. I've given most of the money to them.'

'That's a... a kind thing to have done,' said Rolanda, drinking the rest of her champagne in one gulp and refilling the glass.

'Yes,' her father agreed.

'Right, well. I have to go,' said Desiree, 'but I'm so glad we're on speaking terms again. I'll come round next Sunday and take the girls to the park, would that be okay?'

'Um... next Sunday?' Her father stood up. 'No, we're busy. We're going to see a friend.'

'Oh, okay, on the Saturday then?' she suggested, half knowing he would say they were busy, but the other half of her wanting to prove herself wrong—prove that he did love her and miss her, and want to be a part of her life now, with or without the three million.

'Sorry,' said Rolanda, 'we already have something booked for the Saturday.'

'Okay, never mind, let me know what suits you and I'll arrange to take a day off work,' said Desiree. She hated the feeling of desperation tearing her up inside.

'What Rolanda is trying to say is, we don't think it would be a good idea for you to come round again. Whenever you do, it ends up in an argument, and we don't want the children seeing that.'

'But... But today hasn't ended in an argument. Look, we're being perfectly civil, aren't we?'

Both her father and Rolanda were now standing up.

'Girls, go and play in the playroom, please,' said her father.

The girls smiled at Desiree and ran into the other room.

'You haven't changed, Desi. You're still the same. Selfish. Thinking only of yourself,' he said.

'We don't want your influence on our children,' sneered Rolanda.

'See? Another argument is brewing,' said her father.

Desiree shook her head. 'Suits me fine,' she said, a lump forming in her throat, tears threatening to fall.

She left the house, the stares of her father and Rolanda burning into her back.

Once outside, her tears began to fall. She continued to walk away, confused at why she felt so upset. Wasn't it better that she'd seen their true colours? She tried to shake off the painful memories, ruing her decision to visit them today. Why did it matter so much to have their approval?

She tried to focus on thoughts of the girls, Erina and Jessica. She'd enjoyed seeing them, even though the visit was cut short. Her wish was that the money she'd won would benefit them in the future, and make up in some small way for her not being able to be there for them.

Walking back to the Tube station Desiree felt exhausted and regretted making the journey on her own. She should have taken a taxi, or asked her mother to drive her. The last thing she wanted was to faint again and end up in hospital. But this illness made her want to be a part of this sorry city. She wanted to walk the weatherworn streets, wanted to ride on the crowded Tube trains with the unfriendly passengers, to embrace it all, because she didn't know how long she had left.

The twenty minute train ride left her light-headed. She couldn't wait to exit the station into the fresh air, even if it was cold. At least she had her new warm coat to keep the wind from biting. She focussed on getting indoors, making a hot drink.

The journey took more of a toll than she had appreciated, and with every step she could feel herself growing weaker. *I just have to make it to the door... Nearly there...*

Desiree collapsed three doors away from her house. A passerby called an ambulance when he found her, about ten minutes later. Too late to save her. She had lost too much blood, having hit her head when she fell against the corner of a sharp stone wall leading into a driveway.

A pool of blood had formed around her, and where the early evening sun reflected off the thick liquid, the colour shone a bright red, matching her coat.

More books by Maria Savva:

Novels:

Coincidences
A Time to Tell
Second Chances
The Dream
Haunted

Novella:

Cutting The Fat (co-author: Jason McIntyre)

Short Story Collections:

Pieces of a Rainbow
Love and Loyalty (and Other Tales)
Fusion
Delusion and Dreams
3

Find out more about the author and where to buy her books, on her official website: http://www.MariaSavva.com